The Alaskan Adventure

Across the clearing, the four wolves stood like statues, tongues lolling from the sides of their mouths. Frank wondered if they were laughing at the expressions on the faces of their prey.

"Any ideas, Frank?" Joe muttered out of the side of his mouth.

"Tell them we come in peace and ask them to take us to their leader," Frank muttered back.

"Thanks a bunch," Joe said. "Any *good* ideas?".

"Let's see what happens if we back off," Frank suggested. "Slowly."

Together, the two brothers took a cautious step backward, then another. As if they'd been choreographed, the wolves began to move in the same instant. Two peeled off to the left and two to the right.

"Are they giving up?" Joe asked.

"In your dreams," Frank replied. "They're starting to circle us. That means t[...] pack attack mode. . . ."

The Hardy Boys Mystery Stories

Available from MINSTREL Books

THE HARDY BOYS®

138

THE ALASKAN ADVENTURE

FRANKLIN W. DIXON

A MINSTREL® BOOK

Published by POCKET BOOKS
New York London Toronto Sydney Tokyo Singapore

A MINSTREL PAPERBACK *Original*

 A Minstrel Book published by
POCKET BOOKS, a division of Simon & Schuster Inc.
1230 Avenue of the Americas, New York, NY 10020

Copyright © 1996 by Simon & Schuster Inc.

Front cover illustration by Lee MacLeod

Produced by Mega-Books, Inc.

All rights reserved, including the right to reproduce
this book or portions thereof in any form whatsoever.
For information address Pocket Books, 1230 Avenue
of the Americas, New York, NY 10020

ISBN: 0-671-50524-6

First Minstrel Books printing June 1996

10 9 8 7 6 5 4 3 2 1

THE HARDY BOYS MYSTERY STORIES is a trademark
of Simon & Schuster Inc.

THE HARDY BOYS, A MINSTREL BOOK and colophon
are registered trademarks of Simon & Schuster Inc.

Printed in the U.S.A.

Contents

THE
ALASKAN
ADVENTURE

1 A Thousand Feet Down

The bush plane banked into a steep left turn. Seventeen-year-old Joe Hardy jammed his boots against the firewall and grabbed the handle over his head. He was looking out the side window straight down for a thousand feet.

"That's Glitter up ahead," Flip Atkins, the pilot, said, gesturing with his thumb.

Joe stared down at the landscape, looking for the town. Trees stretched as far as he could see in every direction. A broad white swathe cut through them like an enormous highway. That, Joe knew, was the Yukon River. The ice covering it was ten feet thick at this time of year. Then he saw Glitter. It was facing the river, looking like a cluster of toy buildings in a clearing. That was

1

where Joe and his older brother, Frank, were going.

"Okay!" Joe exclaimed. "This is going to be fantastic!"

Flip grinned. "This is real bush country," he said. "You don't have to worry about the neighbors bothering you because there aren't any."

"I can see why people call Alaska the Big Land," Frank said from the rear seat. "I don't see the airstrip, though."

Flip's grin widened. "Sure you do," he replied. "It's right down there—a mile wide and two thousand miles long."

"We're going to land on the ice?" Joe asked. "Isn't the surface too rough for that?"

"It would be," Flip said with a nod. "But come winter, the folks here smooth off a stretch of the ice for me." The plane leveled off, then the nose dipped.

"See those two lines of trees?" Flip added. "They're stuck in the ice to mark where it's been smoothed. As long as we go right down between them, we'll be fine."

Flip adjusted the throttle and lowered the flaps to slow the plane for landing.

Joe's stomach lurched when they hit an air pocket. He decided this wasn't the time to bug

Flip with more questions. He looked over his shoulder at Frank and said, "This is going to be a real adventure, isn't it? And it'll be great to see David again."

Frank smiled. "It sure will."

David Natik was an Athabascan, a Native American, and had lived his whole life in the tiny town below them. As part of a sports exchange program sponsored by the Bureau of Indian Affairs, he had spent several weeks living with the Hardy family in Bayport, New York, during football season. Now Joe and Frank were returning the visit during spring break. They were going to have just enough time to help David get ready for the famous Iditarod Dog Sled Race and then see him start the race in Anchorage. They were flying back to New York from there.

"Hang on," Flip said. He angled the plane downward.

Joe tightened his grip on the handle overhead. As far as he was concerned, it wasn't the plane that was going down. It was the whole big earth coming up.

Flip reduced power still more, pulled back on the stick to raise the nose, then pushed it forward a little. As the landing skis touched the river ice, he reversed the prop pitch and gunned the throttle. The engine roared, the plane vibrated and bounced, and then, in what seemed like no

3

more than a breath or two, it was over. The plane came to a stop. Flip reached down and switched off the motor. The sudden, deep silence almost hurt Joe's ears.

"You'd better zip up your parkas," Flip said as he reached for the door handle. "The cold around here is sneaky. It's never windy, so you might think it's not cold at all. But it's way below zero, all the same."

Frank and Joe zipped up, then climbed out.

"Do you think they know we're here?" Joe asked, his breath turning frosty white in the sparkling air.

"They know, all right," Flip replied. "That's why I buzzed the town." He opened the baggage compartment, hauled out the Hardys' duffel bags, and set them on the ice.

"Glitter's a funny name for a Native American town," Frank remarked.

Flip began to pull cartons and packages from the freight compartment. "Back in the Gold Rush days," he said, "about a hundred years ago, there were thousands of miners and prospectors back in these hills. They called the town Glitter because of the old saying."

He paused and glanced at the Hardys.

"All that glitters is not gold," Frank and Joe said together.

4

"Yup, that's the one," Flip said. "From what the old-timers say, this was some lively spot, too. But then the gold petered out. Practically all of the miners left. About the only people who stayed were the Athabascans, who'd been in these parts all along."

"Look, Frank!" Joe cried, pointing toward the riverbank. "Isn't that David?"

"Sure looks like him," Frank replied with excitement in his voice.

About fifty yards away a sturdy figure of medium height was scrambling down the riverbank onto the ice. The hood of his fur parka was thrown back, and Joe recognized the broad face, high cheekbones, and black hair of their friend.

Joe and Frank grabbed their gear and hurried across the frozen river to meet him.

"Welcome to Alaska," David called. They shook hands and slapped one another on the back. "How was the trip?"

"Pretty long," Frank said. "The last leg was the most fun."

"Come on, we'll drop your stuff off, then I'll show you around," David said.

Now that they were on the ground, Joe could see that the town was built on low ground between two hillsides. The scattered log cabins seemed to hunker down against the penetrating

5

cold. Plumes of white smoke rose straight from metal stovepipes poking into the deep blue Arctic sky.

"I got the stove going in your cabin," David told them as they followed him into the town. "I hope it's okay. I'm just down the way, with my uncle Peter and aunt Mona—the Windmans. I've been living with them while my mom and dad are down in Fairbanks. They're working in a snowshoe factory."

Joe spotted a wooden sign on the wall of the only two-story building in sight. "'General Store, J. Ferguson, proprietor,'" he read aloud. "It sounds like something out of the Old West."

"It is." David laughed. "Except we've got Flip's airplane, instead of stagecoaches and wagon trains. Everything is flown in from Fairbanks. Whatever you need, if you can't get it from Jake, you have to do without it."

Out on the river Flip revved up the engine of the plane for takeoff. They turned to look.

"There he goes," David said. "He's going to drop off the mail downriver, the same way he did here. He comes by once a week."

The plane sped over the ice between the two rows of spruce trees and lifted off like a Canada goose, then turned westward.

As they walked through the town, David pointed to a white building with small windows.

6

"That's the assembly room," he explained. "In the old days it was a dance hall. Now we use it for town meetings and stuff like that."

Two big posters were tacked to the bulletin board next to the entrance. One was professionally printed. A Yes Vote Is a Vote for Glitter's Future, it read. The other, hand lettered on a ragged piece of cardboard, read Save Our Town—Vote No.

"What's going on?" Frank asked, gesturing toward the posters.

"There's a big vote coming up," David told him. "A company called ThemeLife wants to turn Glitter into a tourist attraction."

"Like Disney World?" Joe asked. He glanced around at the tumbledown cabins.

David laughed. "That's the general idea," he said. "It's kind of hard to imagine, isn't it?"

"How do people feel about it?" Frank asked.

David shrugged. "Pretty mixed. Some people are for it, some not."

Up ahead, a man with tangled gray hair and a long gray beard shuffled past on a crosspath. Joe noticed that his green parka and heavy wool pants were roughly patched. "Who was that?" Joe asked David in a low voice.

"Oh, that's Lucky Moeller," David replied. "He works a gold claim a little ways outside of town. He's sort of a character."

7

"He doesn't look like someone who struck it rich," Frank observed.

David smiled. "Not yet, anyway. But give him time. He's only been at it for forty or fifty years."

Joe and Frank followed David through the town. As they neared the outskirts, David pointed to one of the cabins and said, "That's the Windman cabin—where my aunt and uncle and my cousin, Justine, live. They wanted to come with me to meet you, but they had to gather firewood. We'll see them later. And this is where you'll be staying."

He led them to a small cabin a dozen yards from the Windman cabin and pushed the door open. Inside were two bunks piled high with blankets, a table and chairs, and an old potbellied stove. A bearskin rug lay on the floor, and the woodbox next to the stove was stacked with split logs.

"It's pretty rough," David said. "Not like what you're used to back in Bayport."

"It's great," Frank assured him, tossing his duffel down on one of the bunks. "Warm and cozy. Don't worry about us. Joe and I have been in places a lot rougher."

"You can say that again" Joe said.

David gave him a relieved look. He'd obviously been worried, Joe thought, about how his friends from the Lower Forty-Eight were going to handle a visit to the Alaskan bush.

"You want to see my sled dogs?" he asked.

"Cool," Joe said.

The three friends left the cabin and sauntered to the edge of the town. As they neared a cluster of doghouses, a loud chorus of barking greeted them. What seemed like dozens of thick-furred huskies jumped to their feet, their tails wagging.

"These aren't all yours, are they?" Joe asked, amazed.

"Oh, yes, they are," David told him. "I've got twenty-one sled dogs. But I'll be using just twelve of them in the Iditarod. It's too bad you won't have time to see more of the race."

"I wish we could. But we've got to get back to school," Frank said.

"Yeah," Joe said. "Believe me, I wish we could postpone school. I'd love to see the finish of the race."

"Most people see only a small part of the race," David said. "It's long—eleven hundred miles, all the way from Anchorage to Nome."

Joe stared at him. "Eleven hundred miles!" he repeated, astonished.

David stopped next to a dog that had been watching every move they made. "This is Iron-heart," he said. He squatted down and hugged a powerful gray-and-white husky with glacial blue eyes. Ironheart wagged his tail. "Ironheart's my lead dog."

Ironheart began to lick his master's face. David laughed and pulled away.

"The lead dog is the most important part of the team," David added. "If we run into a whiteout, Ironheart's a lot more important than I am."

"What's a whiteout?" Frank asked.

"That's when a blizzard blows up on the trail," David explained. "It can get so thick, you can't see your hand in front of your face. It's really dangerous. But a really good lead dog like Ironheart has an instinct that tells him where the trail is and alerts him to dangers like thin river ice. I'd never do a race like the Iditarod without him."

"How long does it take?" Frank asked.

"That depends," David said. He went around the pack of dogs, giving each one a pat on the head. "The winners usually do it in eleven or twelve days. It has to be the most grueling race around."

"It must be hard on the dogs," Joe said.

"Oh, no. They love it," David told him. "Especially when it's twenty degrees below zero, so they don't overheat. They can hardly wait to go mushing."

"Mushing? Sounds like soggy oatmeal to me," Joe said.

David smiled. "That's what we call dog-sledding. It comes from the French word *marcher*. It means 'let's get going.'"

"Do you have a team supporting you?" Frank asked.

David shook his head. "Nope. In the Iditarod, you race alone. And you have to carry everything you need, too: food for you and your dogs, clothes, emergency supplies—everything."

Joe said, "That seems like a pretty strict rule."

"I know," David said. "But it all goes back to 1925, when there was an epidemic of diphtheria in Nome and the town ran out of medicine. There wasn't a road, and airplanes couldn't get through, either. But some of the best dogsled mushers in Alaska carried the medicine from Anchorage to Nome, through blizzards and all, and got there in time to save the town. The Iditarod is like a memorial to them."

"Hey, wait a minute," Frank said. "When you were staying with us, we took you to Central Park, in New York City, because you wanted to see a statue of a sled dog."

David smiled. "That's right," he said. "That was Balto, a lead dog who was one of the heroes of the rescue of Nome."

11

He bent down to pet Ironheart again. "And *my* lead dog is just as great as Balto, aren't you, fellow? We're going to win the Iditarod and take home the fifty-thousand-dollar prize."

Joe blew out a frosty whistle. "Fifty thousand dollars? Sign me up—I'll pull the sled myself!"

"You wouldn't get very far without a dog team," David said, laughing. "And the competition's pretty fierce."

As the three were walking back into town, Joe saw a young man about their age. Like David, he was dressed in wool pants and a fur parka, but he had the hood up and his head down, as if he didn't want to be noticed.

"That's Gregg Anderson," David said. He called out, "Hey, Gregg, come say hello to my friends from back east."

Gregg stopped but didn't speak.

"Gregg's running the Iditarod, too," David continued. "It's the first time for both of us. The town's pretty excited about us two."

Gregg glared at him. "You think you and your team are pretty good, don't you?" he said. "I know you've beat me a few times. But I'll tell you one thing. Maybe I won't win the Iditarod this time. But neither will you. I'm going to finish way ahead of you. Nothing's going to stop me. I swear it."

2 "Hike! Hike!"

Tight-lipped and scowling, Gregg pushed past Frank and walked quickly up the path. Frank watched him for a few moments, then turned to David. "What's that guy's problem?" he asked. "Is he always like that?"

David shrugged. "Sort of. We used to be friends when we were little, but not anymore. I guess it burns him that my dog team usually beats his."

Joe pushed David lightly on the shoulder. "Maybe you're just a better musher."

David playfully shoved him back. "Hey," he said, "you're learning the language."

The path they were on took them past an open yard that contained a big stack of fifty-five-gallon

13

metal drums and a small shack. Frank heard a mechanical hum coming from the shack and asked David about it.

"That's the town generator," David explained. "The diesel oil to power it is brought in by barge during the summer, before the Yukon ices over. That means we have to be careful about how we use electricity. If the oil runs low before the spring thaw, we're out of luck."

Frank glanced around. He'd never really thought about how isolated David's town was. As long as nothing went wrong, life was probably as secure here as anywhere. But even the smallest emergency could be enough to push the town to the brink of disaster.

As they walked on, Frank found himself thinking about Gregg and his determination to finish ahead of David in the Iditarod. You needed to look out for somebody with that kind of intensity.

"David?" Frank said. "Has that guy Gregg ever given you any trouble?"

David looked over his shoulder and said, "Not really. His bark's worse than his bite."

Joe grinned. "Maybe that's a good thing for a dogsled driver," he cracked.

David grinned back. "Gregg wants to be first in everything," he said. "But life's not like that."

14

"Has he ever beaten you in a race?" Frank asked.

"He's come pretty close," David replied.

"Yeah, but close only counts in horseshoes and hand grenades," Joe said, quoting one of her father's favorite sayings.

They all laughed. But Frank knew that the bigger the race, the bigger the temptation. And the Iditarod was the biggest dogsled race of all. Not only that, everybody in Glitter must be rooting for one or the other of the two hometown mushers. That could put an enormous amount of pressure on a guy like Gregg. Enough pressure to make him try something underhanded against his rival, David?

As they turned onto another dirt road, Frank saw a tall man in a green parka and green twill pants coming toward them.

"Oh, there's Curt Stone. He's the guy from the company," David told them.

"What company?" Frank asked, noticing the confident way the man walked.

"ThemeLife—the company I told you about, which wants to turn Glitter into a theme park," David replied. "He's been coming here all winter, talking to people and trying to convince them to vote for the plan."

Stone walked up to them with a smile. "Hello,

15

David," he said. "And these must be your friends from New York."

"That's right, Mr. Stone," David said.

The man shook his head. "Just call me Curt, David," he said.

David introduced Frank and Joe. "They're here to visit and to help me get ready for the Iditarod," he explained.

"So I heard." Curt gave Frank and Joe a friendly smile and said, "Welcome to Alaska. One thing you fellows will have to get used to— this may be a big country, but news travels faster here than anywhere I've ever been. I hope you have a good stay. You can count on David to take good care of you." He walked away.

"He seems like a nice guy," Joe remarked as the three continued on their way. "This project must be pretty important for him to spend so much time in your town."

David nodded. "I guess so," he said. "Or maybe he just likes it here. Why shouldn't he? *I* do."

Frank saw the cabin where he and Joe would be staying up ahead. He didn't yet have a good mental map of the area, but with the river along one side and the forest on the other three sides, getting oriented would be pretty easy.

"Oh," David said, sounding disappointed. "The curtains are still closed at Aunt Mona and

Uncle Peter's. I was sure they'd be back by now. I wanted you to meet them. Oh, well—later for that. Hey, are you guys tired? Do you need to take a rest or anything?"

Frank glanced over at Joe, then said, "No, we're fine. But if there's something you've got to do . . ."

"It's not that," David said. "I was wondering if maybe you'd like to go for a ride."

"You mean, with the dogs?" Joe asked eagerly. David nodded.

"Believe it!" Joe said. "When?"

"How about right now?"

"You're on!" cried Joe. The walk back to the huskies seemed to take much less time. Once there, Frank and Joe helped David carry a sturdy oak sled from a storage shed. They set it on a flat piece of ground next to the trail.

"It's so long," Joe said, sounding surprised.

"That's to hold supplies," David explained, "and it's long enough to sleep on, too, when you're on the trail."

He started laying out a long series of connected harnesses. The huskies began barking eagerly and leaping up, then falling back as they reached the end of the ropes that kept them close to their houses.

"You want to help hitch them up?" David asked. "Here, we'll bring them to the sled one by one, in order. The ones closest to the sled are called the wheel dogs. We'll take them over first."

David grabbed one of the huskies, untied him, and led him to the slot just in front of the sled. The dog stood quietly while David put the padded harness around his powerful chest.

"You have to let them know you're in charge," David said. "Once they know you mean business, they're fine. Joe, why don't you bring Big Foot over? And Frank, you can fetch Gray Dawn."

Frank and Joe went over to the dogs David pointed out, took them by the collars, and led them to the sled, where David harnessed them. Soon it was the turn of Ironheart, the lead dog. Frank scanned the rig and estimated at least forty feet between Ironheart and the front of the sled. Dogsledding needed a lot of room.

By now the team of huskies had turned into a powerhouse of energy and enthusiasm. Tails wagging, the eager dogs jumped up against the harnesses, ready to get moving. This was what they lived for. This was what they loved.

"They need a good run," David said. "You two will take the place of the weight of the supplies."

Joe sat in the seat, while Frank squeezed in front of Joe. David stood at the rear of the sled, next to the runners.

18

"What, no steering wheel?" Joe called out. "No accelerator?"

"No seat belt or airbag?" Frank added.

They all laughed.

Ironheart looked over his shoulder at his master and panted. It looked to Frank as if the husky, too, was enjoying the joke.

"Here we go," David said. "Hike! Hike!" he shouted at the dogs.

The huskies dug their feet into the packed snow of the trail and lunged forward. The sled was soon bouncing along a rutted path toward the river. Frank and Joe were so startled at the sudden speed of the team that neither of them said a word.

"Hike! Hike!" David called again.

Frank glanced back at him. David had his left foot resting on the runner. With his right he kicked at the trail to help push the team along.

Frank fastened the neck tab on his parka and pulled the hood tighter around his ears. The icy wind had already numbed his nose and cheeks. The path plunged down the riverbank and onto the ice. For a moment the sled felt as if it had become airborne. Frank grabbed the sides of the sled.

Behind him Joe shouted, "Waa-hoo!"

As the dogs felt the sled move onto the slicker

surface of the river ice, they picked up the pace. "Hold on!" David shouted.

The white expanses of snow and ice glittered blindingly in the winter sunlight. Frank narrowed his eyes to slits and looked around. The wild silence of unending Alaska surrounded them. Nothing broke the stillness but the steady high-pitched hissing of the sled runners on the ice.

Just ahead the trail branched. "Gee!" David called out to Ironheart. "Gee!"

Ironheart led the team to the right.

Frank turned halfway around and asked, "What do you say for left?"

"Haw," David replied. "That's one of the first things a sled dog has to learn."

"This is *so cool!*" Joe exclaimed.

"Yeah," David answered. "About twenty degrees below zero."

They laughed as the team continued angling diagonally across the Yukon. The trail looked well worn. Frank wondered if this was where David did most of his training for the Iditarod. But there must be other mushers in town, too, who used the same dogsled trails to collect firewood from across the river or to do other errands. The Yukon really was a highway, winter and summer alike.

"We've got company," David said.

Frank and Joe looked around.

"Off to the left," David added. "It's Gregg."

Frank craned his neck and saw another dog team moving along the river, on a trail closer to the bank. "Is he trying to race you?" he asked.

"No, just out giving his team a run," David told him.

"Funny coincidence that he's doing it right now," Joe said. "He's moving pretty fast, isn't he?"

David looked over again, then said, "I don't think he's carrying a load. That's not the way I train a team, but I guess he has his own ideas."

Frank twisted to get a better look at Gregg and his dogs. As he did, something else caught his eye. "David?" he called. "What's that smoke in the town?"

David looked over his shoulder. "Whoa!" he shouted. "Whoa!" The sled lurched as he jammed his foot on the blade brake, which dug into the snow-packed trail.

Ironheart and the rest of the team stopped.

"Something's wrong," David said as he studied the column of black smoke rising from the edge of town.

"What is it?" Joe said.

"We'd better get back fast," David said. "That looks to me like Uncle Peter's cabin."

21

3 Throwing Snow on Fire

David ran toward the head of the dog team. As he passed the sled, he yelled, "Come on! Lift the sled. I'm going to turn the team around."

Frank and Joe climbed out on either side of the sled and followed David as he ran.

David grabbed Ironheart's harness and led him around in a wide circle over the rough ice. The team followed, then stopped. Frank and Joe hoisted the sled into the air and carefully maneuvered it in a half turn that left it facing back toward Glitter.

As the Hardys were clambering back into their places on the sled, David grabbed the handhold and started to push. "Ironheart!" he shouted. "Hike! Hike!"

Ironheart leaned into the straps around his muscular chest and dug his paws into the trail. The rest of the team did the same. They surged forward.

Downriver the smoke from the Windman cabin smeared the sky with an ugly black blotch.

David pushed the team to full speed. "Pull, Ironheart! Pull! Pull!"

Ironheart strained against the harness. He and the other dogs seemed as aware of the emergency as David and the Hardys.

"What do you think happened?" Frank asked.

"I don't know," David replied. "It could be anything. But fire is about the worst thing that can happen. The whole town is made of wood."

Frank noticed Gregg across the ice, still mushing his team away from town. "We should tell him about the fire," he said, pointing.

"He won't hear us," David said. "Wait until we get closer."

They raced along the slick ice trail, skimming over the frozen river. When they had shortened the distance, David shouted, "Gregg!"

His rival didn't even turn his head.

"Gregg! Gregg!" David called again.

Gregg ignored him and continued driving his team away from town.

23

"I guess he didn't hear us," David said.

Frank wasn't so sure about that. On the frozen flat river nothing stopped sound from traveling a long way. Frank thought Gregg was pretending not to notice, as a way of showing his resentment toward David. He didn't realize that David was trying to alert him to an emergency.

Ironheart led the team up the riverbank. When they reached a flat spot near the cabin, David stopped the team and Frank and Joe jumped out of the sled.

By now the townspeople had formed a bucket brigade between the cabin and another one nearby that had a cistern full of water inside. Three men came running up with a long hose connected to a hand pump.

"No fire trucks?" Joe asked, looking around.

"Nothing," David said.

The men and women handed sloshing buckets along the line. A broad-shouldered man at the end of the line took each bucket in turn, threw the water onto the flames, then tossed the empty bucket to someone in the second line to be handed back and refilled.

"Here, take these," David said. He grabbed two snow shovels and tossed them to Frank and Joe and took a third one for himself. "Throw snow on the fire. My aunt and uncle are over there"—he pointed with the shovel—"we'll talk to them later."

Frank threw one shovelful of snow after another through the gaping window of the cabin. It was heavy work. His panting breaths formed a dense white cloud that left a rim of ice particles on his eyelashes. Next to him Joe grunted as he tossed each new load of snow. Others had joined in by now, and the burning cabin was surrounded by a wall of firefighters.

At last Frank realized he was no longer looking at flames, only billowing white smoke. The Arctic cold, which had been kept away by the heat of the fire, rushed back in. Frank felt a shiver that started in the small of his back and traveled right up his backbone.

As the townspeople realized they had won the battle against the fire, a cheer went up. Frank, Joe, and David exchanged wide grins and pounded one another on the back.

Then David took the Hardys over to meet his aunt Mona, uncle Peter, and cousin Justine. They looked stricken. Everything they had in the world now lay in charred ruins.

"I'm sorry about the fire, Mrs. Windman," Frank said.

David's aunt managed a weak smile. "Thank you. Please call us Mona and Peter. We're not formal up here," she said. "I'm sorry, too. I'm afraid we can't do much to welcome you to Glitter," she went on. "We don't even know where we'll sleep tonight."

David gave her a quick hug. "Don't worry about that," he said. "You can use Mom and Dad's cabin until you rebuild yours."

David's uncle went over to the doorway, peered inside the cabin, and then returned.

"How's it look, Dad?" Justine asked. She looked as if she was about thirteen.

"The worst of it is in the back," Peter reported. "I think we can save most of the clothes and furniture and stuff."

"It'll need a lot of airing out," Justine said. "It really stinks."

"I'll get the stove going at our place," David said. "Then I have to take care of my team."

"Can we help?" Joe asked.

David shook his head. "No, thanks, I'm fine," he said. He went down the path to a cabin just beyond the one where Frank and Joe were staying.

Frank turned his attention back to Peter. "How did the fire start?" he asked.

"I don't know," Peter replied, shaking his head. "We were out gathering firewood, and when we got back, I saw the glow through the

26

windows. It wasn't a chimney fire, that's one thing I know."

"How?" Joe asked.

Before Peter could answer, Justine whispered, "Daddy, watch out. Here comes Willy Ekus."

Peter's face tightened. "Let him come," he said.

Frank glanced around. The man who was coming toward them had an odd, lopsided smile on his face. That, and his slow, almost aimless walk, made him look, as Frank's father would say, "a few bricks shy of a load." But there was a shrewd glint in his eye that made Frank wonder if it might be an act.

"Too bad about your cabin, Peter," Willy said in a singsong voice. "I guess you'll have to build a new one now. But you're good at building cabins, aren't you? You're better at that than at trapping, aren't you? Maybe you should give up trapping and just build cabins, Peter. Too bad if they burn down, but then you can build another one, can't you, Peter?"

"You listen here, Willy," Peter began. He took a step toward the other man. Frank tensed up, ready to help break up a fight if one started.

"Too bad about your cabin," Willy said again, with the same steady, lopsided smile. "You'll have to spend all your time building a new one.

27

Not much time for trapping. Not much time at all."

Peter scowled at him. "Willy?" he said tautly. "Did you have anything to do with the fire?"

"Yes, I did," Willy said. "I helped put it out. I passed the buckets. I wanted to help, even if you are working a trapline that belongs to me. I guess you won't be working it for a while, will you?" he added with a giggle.

Frank looked over at Joe, who rolled his eyes.

"Do you know how the fire got started?" Peter continued. "If you do, you'd better tell me."

"Maybe a match, maybe a torch, maybe a lamp that fell over," Willy replied. "Too bad about your cabin, Peter. But that's the way things go. Now you'll have to build another one, instead of poaching on another man's trapline."

He turned and walked away. Peter started after him, but Mona grabbed his arm and held him back.

"No," she said. "Leave him be. Let's get inside, out of the cold. I'll make a pot of tea, then we can think about dinner."

As they walked up the path toward the cabin, Justine said to Frank and Joe, "Willy and Dad have been arguing about that trapline for years. I wish they'd quit it. And now they've got that ThemeLife plan to argue about, too. Did David tell you about that?"

"Uh-huh," Joe replied. "What does your dad think about it?"

"He's against it," Justine told him. "He says if it goes through, we'll be like animals in the circus, showing off for visitors instead of being free to live our lives the way we always have."

Frank asked, "What about Willy? Why is he for it?"

"Who knows why Willy does anything? He's weird," Justine said. "He always has been. Maybe he's for the plan because my dad is against it."

"Do you think Willy's weird enough to set fire to your cabin?" Joe asked her.

She looked at him with wide eyes. "Nobody's that crazy!" she exclaimed. "Look around—the whole town's made of wood. If there'd been any wind, all of Glitter could have burnt down. And then none of us would make it through the winter."

David's parents' cabin was still a little chilly, but Frank could feel the warmth radiating from the cast-iron woodstove. Mona took off her parka and hung it on a peg behind the door, then poured water from a five-gallon can into a kettle and put it on top of the stove to heat.

"I'll bring more water from the spring," Justine said, picking up two empty cans.

"Let us help," Joe said, reaching for one of the cans.

29

Justine smiled. "It's okay," she said. "I'll use the sledge. It's no trouble at all. I do it all the time."

As she went out the door, David came in. "Well, guys," he said to Frank and Joe, "you're getting a pretty rough introduction to our way of life up here."

"Rougher than you know," Mona remarked. "While you were gone, Willy came by and tried to pick a fight with your uncle."

"What about?" David asked. "The ThemeLife plan?"

"Not this time," Mona replied. "I'll say this, though. I'll be glad when the voting is over with. It's been going on too long, and it's dividing the town. Everybody's getting mad at everybody else. That's no way to live."

"Which side seems to be winning?" Frank asked.

Peter shrugged. "We won't know until the vote on Friday," he said. "A lot of people don't want to say what they think."

"Jake Ferguson won't say which way he plans to vote," Mona said. "He's so money hungry, I guess he's afraid he'll lose customers if he takes sides."

"People around here have to buy at the store and pay Jake's prices, whether they like what he thinks or not," Peter pointed out.

"What about Gregg?" Joe asked.

David smiled. "The only thing Gregg thinks about these days is coming in ahead of me in the Iditarod," he said. "But his dad, Reeve, is pretty tight with Willy, so I wouldn't be surprised if they're for the plan, too."

"I've tried talking to Reeve," Peter said. "He won't say much, but I didn't feel I was getting through to him. Too bad. People think nothing will change except that they'll start making a lot of money."

Frank glanced out the window at the back of the cabin. The edge of the dark forest loomed just a few yards away. How hard would it have been for someone to slip out of the woods and put some kind of firebomb inside Mona and Peter's cabin, then escape unnoticed into the woods?

Frank was turning to ask Peter about the damage inside the cabin when he was startled by a loud crash. Mona let out a scream as broken glass sprayed across the room from a shattered window.

31

4 Changes for the Better?

Without thinking, Joe flung up his arm to protect his face. Shards of glass showered him and tinkled to the floor. At the same moment he heard a thump. A charred log, about two feet long and three inches in diameter, rolled past him and across the floor. Someone had hurled it through the window. Joe grabbed his parka and ran for the door.

Outside, the only person in sight was Justine. She was about twenty yards up the path, pulling a loaded sledge toward the house.

"Did you see anyone just now?" Joe called out to her.

"No," she called back. "Is something wrong? What happened?"

Frank dashed out of the house and stopped next to Joe. "Did you see him?" he demanded.

Joe shook his head. "No. He could be anywhere by now."

"I don't like this a bit," Frank said. "It's lucky nobody was hurt."

Justine ran up to them, just as Peter and David came running outside. Peter was holding a piece of firewood like a club.

"He got away," Frank said, his voice full of disgust.

David told Justine what had just happened.

"That's terrible!" Justine said, her eyes blazing. "What's happening to our town? Everyone's turning on one another like wild animals!"

Peter looked down at the log in his hand, as if he didn't remember how it got there. Then he sighed and said, "We'd better cover that broken window with something before the cabin freezes." He led the group inside.

While Peter and David taped a sheet of black plastic over the gaping window, Mona swept up the broken glass. She made the pot of tea, and they all sat down to drink it.

"David's parents cleaned out the cupboards before they went to Fairbanks," Mona said.

"There's not much to eat here. We'll have to lay in some groceries. I'll make a list."

Frank stirred his tea to cool it, then cleared his throat and said, "We still don't know how the fire started. But we do know the log didn't fly through the window on its own. Somebody threw it. Any idea who?"

"If I knew for sure," Peter growled, "I wouldn't be sitting here. I'd be going after him."

"A lot of things like this have been going on," Justine said. "Crazy things. Things that shouldn't happen."

"That's true," David said. "People in town have been having more accidents than usual. And it's getting worse."

"So you're not the only targets?" Frank asked.

Justine gave him a serious look. "David told us about you and Joe," she said. "He said you've solved all kinds of mysteries. Do you think you can solve this one?"

"We don't have a police department in town, any more than we have a fire department," Mona said, looking up from her grocery list.

"If we need the police, we call in for state troopers," Justine added. "But we never need them."

"We'll do our best," Frank promised them. "What about the accidents? Is there any pattern to them?"

"Life isn't easy out here in the Alaskan bush, Frank. You've already seen that," David said. "We're always near the edge of disaster. And we don't have a lot of the safety nets you're used to in the Lower Forty-Eight. No water system, no hospital or doctor for a hundred miles or more."

"What David's getting at," Mona said, "is that we shrug off things. We don't even remember them a week later. But if somebody set our cabin on fire, that's not something we can shrug off."

"Can you think of anybody who has a grudge against you?" Joe asked.

"Willy Ekus," Mona and Justine said promptly.

"He's been fighting with Peter over that trapline for ten years or more," Mona added.

Peter looked troubled. "Willy's crazy enough to do it," he admitted. "But I don't think he's got the nerve. He's all talk. What I'm thinking is, you make a lot of money if you do well in the Iditarod. And if David here is upset about what's been happening to us, he's not going to do as well in the race."

"You think Gregg's doing this?" David asked. "If he is, he'd better look out. I'll settle him once and for all!"

"Wait," Frank said. "Peter, I get the idea you're the leader of the group that's against the theme park plan. Do you think that might have something to do with this?"

35

"I don't know," Peter said slowly. "It's pretty clear that Curt Stone's got a lot riding on this plan of his. But I'd hate to think he'd try to burn us out because we're on the other side. He seems like an okay fellow, except for wanting to ruin our town. And even there, he probably thinks he's doing us a favor."

"Maybe Frank and I should do a little poking around," Joe suggested. "Since we're not from around here, maybe people will talk more freely."

David grinned. "You're right—nobody will pay any attention to a couple of *cheechakos.*"

"That means newcomers, right?" Frank asked. "I remember it from a guidebook I was looking at."

"Right," David told him. "And once you've wintered over at least once, you become a sourdough. That comes from the old-time prospectors who made bread from a mixture of flour and water and sourdough starter instead of yeast."

"Speaking of bread," Mona said, "would you mind picking up a few supplies at the general store?" Mona began to clear the teacups from the table. "Here's the list."

"No problem," Joe told her. "That'll give us a good excuse for getting into conversation."

A few minutes later the Hardys left the cabin

36

and started down the path. They hadn't gone very far when a tattered figure in a torn red cap and filthy green parka popped up in front of them.

"You fellows moving in here?" he demanded.

Joe recognized the old prospector they had seen right after their arrival in Glitter. What was his name—Lucky? He didn't look lucky.

"No," Frank answered. "We're friends of David Natik's, up on a visit."

"You looking for gold?" Lucky asked, his head bobbing up and down.

"No, we're here for the race," Joe explained. "The Iditarod."

Lucky glared at him. "You like gold, don't you? Everybody likes gold—gold dust, gold flakes, gold nuggets. I've found them all."

Joe decided to humor him. "That's great," he said. "But we're more interested in the Iditarod. The dogsled race."

"I know all about the Iditarod," Lucky snapped. "David and Gregg are running in it this year. That's a big deal for Glitter, but there's lots of bigger deals, if you know where to look for them."

"Oh? Where's that?" Frank asked.

Lucky tapped his finger against the side of his nose. "That's a secret," he said. "I know a lot of secrets. What about nuggets? You like gold nuggets? Just be careful whose nuggets you put your hands on."

Frank told him, "We're not looking for gold. We're just here to—"

Before Frank could finish his sentence, Lucky turned and walked away. Then he shouted over his shoulder, "Lots of different kinds of gold. You hear that?"

Joe looked over at Frank. "What was that all about?" he asked.

"Gold," Frank replied. "And, like the man said, everybody likes gold, but there're lots of different kinds. I'd say we ought to keep that in mind. Come on, let's see who else we run into."

Joe looked around as they walked through the town. There was a lot of atmosphere to soak up. Two little boys with eyes like black marbles stared at them from the small window of one of the cabins. It occurred to Joe that he and Frank were as exotic a sight for the townspeople as they were to them. A little farther on, an old man whose face had deep wrinkles walked by, bent almost double from the stack of firelogs roped to his back. Two huskies near the door to a cabin rose up and bared their teeth as the Hardys walked by.

"You know," Joe remarked as they neared the

general store, "I thought this theme park idea sounded nutty when David told us about it. But I'm starting to understand why a lot of people might want to come here. It's different."

He and Frank stepped onto the porch of the store and pushed the door open. A bell tinkled, then tinkled again as Joe pushed the door closed behind them.

The general store looked exactly as he had imagined it would. A black potbellied stove stood in the middle of the room, with a couple of battered wooden chairs drawn close to it. The walls were hidden by wooden shelves loaded with canned goods, clocks, hammers, oil lamps, and a hundred other items. Big cloth sacks of flour, rice, and animal feed were stacked in the corners. A tall wooden cabinet with no doors held piles of parkas in all colors, thick woolen shirts, long johns, gloves, socks, and red plaid caps. Near the back were bales of furs, which had been brought in by trappers.

The man who stepped out from behind the counter fit right into the scene. He was about fifty, tall, skinny, and bald, wearing a blue-and-white-striped apron over a shirt and tie.

"You'll be David Natik's friends from New York," he said. "I'm Jake Ferguson. What do you need today?"

Frank handed him the list Mona had drawn up, and Jake began taking items down from the shelves.

"Terrible thing about that fire," he said as he climbed a stepladder to reach some canned goods. "It just shows how important it is to have proper protection. Too bad the town can't afford to have some decent firefighting equipment. Now, if ThemeLife comes in—"

"Are you in favor of the ThemeLife plan, Mr. Ferguson?" Joe asked.

"Call me Jake, son," the man replied. "And as for this big controversy, I guess I'm neutral. I'm a storekeeper. I'll let the others in town battle it out. Whatever they decide is fine with me."

"Oh," Frank said. "From what you said about firefighting equipment, I thought . . ." He let his voice trail off.

Jake gave a little laugh. "Oh, I can't deny that Curt Stone makes some good arguments. His company's done this sort of thing all over the place. They know what pulls people in. They come into a town and emphasize the things that make people want to visit."

He broke off as the bell over the door sounded. A weathered man in a worn parka came in and asked Jake for twenty-five cents' worth of candy from the big jar on the counter.

Jake served him and put the five nickels in his cash drawer. After the man left, he said, "You take Ralph Hunter, who was just in. He's got four kids to feed. If the plan goes through, there'd be new jobs and extra money for people like him."

"Is he voting for ThemeLife?" Frank asked.

Jake paused and looked away. "He's not a good example, I guess," he said, shaking his head. "No, Ralph makes it pretty plain he isn't going to vote yes. But you could argue that he should, for his own good."

While Jake packed Mona's order into two cardboard cartons, Joe and Frank admired a glass case filled with traditional Athabascan handicrafts. "Those are real collector's items," Jake said. "Very expensive. Anything you're interested in?"

Frank laughed. "Just looking, thanks."

Jake totaled the bill and said, "I'll put it on the Windman account. Come see me again. Maybe I'll have something you want to take home as a souvenir."

"Thanks, Jake," Joe said as he and Frank picked up the two cartons of groceries.

When they went outside, Joe saw Curt coming toward them. He waved and smiled. "Well, we *cheechakos* meet again. I hear you went for a dogsled ride. That must have been exciting."

"It was great," Joe said.

41

"Jake has everything, doesn't he?" Curt said. "Even opinions about this and that. It's a wonder he doesn't put a price tag on those, too."

"He was talking about your plans for Glitter," Joe said.

"I hope he had good things to say," Curt replied. "I'm trying to help this town, and it could use help."

"Your company would make a lot of changes, wouldn't it?" Frank asked.

Curt nodded. "Sure. Changes for the better. People are a little nervous about change. I don't blame them. But it's my job to persuade them that they *need* ThemeLife."

"Persuade them how?" asked Joe.

"Why, by explaining the advantages to them," Curt replied. "You'll have to excuse me. I'm due to call in to the home office, and the only way to do that is to use Jake's two-way radio. That's one of the things about Glitter we'll change—we'll bring in modern communications."

Curt went into the store. Joe and Frank headed down the street to the cabin. They hadn't gone far when they heard an anguished cry. They whirled around. Ralph Hunter was on his knees next to a longboat near the river. With another loud cry, he buried his face in his hands and fell forward.

5 Soft Ice Ahead

Frank and Joe set the cartons on the ground and dashed down the icy slope toward the riverbank. Frank scanned the area for some clue to what had happened. There was a crumpled tarp on the ground next to Hunter. It looked as if he had just taken it off the boat. What had he found to cause him such pain?

When they were a few yards away, Joe called, "What's wrong? Can we help?"

Hunter looked up at them and pointed to the bottom of the longboat.

Frank and Joe peered inside. The aluminum hull was riddled with holes from bow to stern.

Hunter shook his head. "It's no good to me

43

now," he said. "I might as well throw it away. What am I going to do come spring?"

Frank estimated that twenty or thirty holes had been punched in the hull. "Who did this?" he asked.

Hunter shook his head again.

A crowd was gathering, drawn by Hunter's cries. At the sight of the damage they murmured to each other. Frank couldn't make out what they were saying.

"I came down and took the cover off, and this is what I found," Hunter said, staring down at the damage. "This boat is all I've got in the world. I depend on it for fishing, once the ice breaks up. How am I going to feed my family now?"

Joe got down on one knee to study the destruction. "Frank," he said, without looking up, "it looks as if this was done with a spike. The holes were punched from inside the boat. Look how clean the edges are."

Frank knelt down and looked at the holes. "You're right," he said. "Whoever did it had to take the cover off first. Pretty risky, unless he did it at night. And in that case, you'd think someone would have heard the hammering."

He straightened up and looked around. Aside from the general store, there were only two cabins nearby. One of them looked closed up, but the other had a faint trail of smoke rising from the chimney.

"Mr. Hunter?" Frank said. "When was the last time you looked at your boat?"

Hunter blinked a couple of times. He seemed a long way off. Frank guessed that he was thinking about the lean summer to come for him and his family.

Frank repeated the question.

"Why, a few days ago," Hunter said. "I don't know . . . Sunday, maybe?"

"You took the tarp off, and it was okay then?" Joe asked.

"That's right," Hunter replied.

Frank asked, "Can you think of any reason someone might want to harm you?"

Hunter got to his feet. "I don't like all these questions," he said. "Everybody's asking me something. Who do I think'll do better in the Iditarod, Gregg Anderson or David Natik? What kind of salmon season do I think we'll have this year? How do I plan to vote at the town meeting? And now you. It's too much."

Frank and Joe stood up, too. "Who's been asking you these questions?" Frank asked. He didn't have much hope that he'd get an answer.

Hunter shook his head. He picked up the tarp and draped it over the longboat. Frank couldn't help thinking that there wasn't much point in protecting the ruined boat.

The crowd of onlookers was beginning to break up. A couple of people came over to Hunter to talk about what had happened. The rest drifted back into the town. Frank noticed one woman go into the nearest cabin.

"Come on," he muttered to Joe. "It's time for us to do a little detecting."

Frank led the way to the little cabin and knocked on the door. The woman opened it.

"What is it?" she asked, looking puzzled.

Frank introduced himself and Joe, then said, "We're trying to find out what happened to Ralph Hunter's longboat. Did you hear any hammering the past few days? Especially at night?"

"Hammering?" the woman repeated. "No, I don't think so. I heard Jake Ferguson out chopping wood a couple of nights ago."

"Is that unusual?" asked Joe.

"I guess it is," she said slowly. "He usually takes care of his woodbox in the daytime. And now that I think of it, he usually uses a chainsaw."

"Did you see him? Or just hear the sounds?" Frank asked.

She shrugged. "I didn't go look. Why should I? Oh—do you think what I heard was somebody wrecking Ralph's longboat?"

46

"It's possible," Joe replied.

"I can't believe it," the woman said, shaking her head.

"Thanks for your help," Frank said. "If you think of anything that might point to who did the damage, will you let us know?"

The woman promised, then closed her door.

Frank and Joe stopped by Jake's store. In response to Joe's question, Jake told them that he hadn't been chopping wood. He hadn't heard anything like that, either, but his bedroom was upstairs at the back, away from the noises of the street.

The Hardys went back and picked up the grocery cartons and started up the hill toward David's family's cabin.

Frank looked around at the empty, snow-packed trail and the tightly closed cabins, and started to laugh. "'Noises of the street'?" he asked, quoting Jake. "Like what—a lonesome elk taking a midnight stroll?"

"It *is* funny," Joe agreed. "But it means that whoever wrecked Hunter's boat could be pretty sure no one would see him do it. Do you think this connects with the fire at Peter's place and the log somebody heaved through the window?"

"If it doesn't, it's quite a coincidence," Frank replied thoughtfully. "When people live in tight quarters like this, cut off from the rest of the

47

world all winter long, it can lead to grudges and feuds that go on for years. Maybe somebody finally cracked and decided to get back at all the people he hates."

"I wonder how Hunter gets along with that guy Willy," Joe said. "I bet David can tell us. In a place like this, everybody knows everything about everybody."

David met them halfway up the hill. "I thought you'd gotten lost," he said.

Joe told him about how Ralph Hunter's boat had been damaged and asked about Willy and Hunter.

"They don't get along at all," David replied. "Haven't for years. But that's not a big surprise. About the only person that Willy *does* get along with is Reeve, Gregg's father."

Frank remembered Hunter's saying that people were asking him questions about the Iditarod. "Does Hunter have a connection to dogsled racing?" he asked.

"Does he!" David cried. "He used to be the best musher for fifty miles around! He still knows more about dogs than practically anyone. But he had to sell his team a few years ago. One of his kids needed an operation."

"That's a shame," Joe said. "But why would people be asking him about this year's race if he won't be in it?"

David looked surprised by the question. "To find out who to bet on," he said. "The Iditarod is the biggest dogsled race there is. There's a lot of money won and lost every year. Some people around here are even making bets on whether Gregg and I finish the race and which of us comes in ahead of the other. I guess if you can't go cheer for your favorite, putting money on him is the next best thing."

They arrived at the cabin and took the groceries inside. Then David said, "What do you say to another training run? My team gets fat and lazy if I don't give them enough exercise."

"Great!" Joe said, answering for both the Hardys.

Frank and Joe helped David harness the team, then they hit the trail. Out on the river the dogs set a fast pace, with their tails curled high and their red tongues hanging out the sides of their mouths.

"Where are we going?" Frank asked.

"Up the Mink River," David replied. He was standing on the rails at the rear of the sled and kicking the trail now and then to help the dogs past a bumpy stretch. "It's not far."

"How far?" Joe asked.

"About five miles. That's not far for this team," David explained.

"Not compared to an eleven-hundred-mile race like the Iditarod, that's for sure," Frank said. "How many dog teams enter the race?"

David paused while the sled bounced over a protruding knot of river ice, then said, "About seventy or eighty."

Frank tried to imagine seventy or eighty teams like David's, maybe a thousand sled dogs, all barking and mushing at once. It was going to be quite a sight when they got to Anchorage.

Frank glanced across the river and said, "I'm surprised there isn't more snow on the hills. Does it melt early?"

"There isn't much to start with," David replied. "It may sound funny, but technically, this region is really a desert. Most years we get less than twelve inches of precipitation."

"Maybe you should trade in your huskies for camels," Joe said.

David smiled. "Not me. I love my dogs." The sled approached a fork in the trail, and he called out, "Ironheart—gee! Gee!"

Ironheart confidently guided the team into the right-hand fork.

A couple of miles farther on, David steered the team off the Yukon and onto a trail that led north on a much smaller river. "This is a shortcut to the Mink River," he explained.

Ten minutes later Frank realized that their pace had slowed to a fast walk.

"I see it," David called out to his lead dog. It was almost as if he had forgotten that Frank and Joe were sitting in the sled.

"See what?" Frank asked.

David hesitated, then said, "Soft ice ahead."

Frank craned his neck. The ice looked fine to him.

"Sometimes a deep spring bubbles up from the stream bed and weakens the ice," David added. "It happens a lot at this time of year."

"What do we do?" Joe asked. "Turn around?"

That wouldn't be easy, Frank realized. The trail they were following on the ice was barely wider than a dogsled. If they tried to get out and turn the sled and team, it would put them right on the thin ice Ironheart had spotted.

"Easy, Ironheart, easy," David called in a soothing voice.

The team was now moving at a bare walk. The huskies looked uneasily from side to side. They must be aware, as Frank and Joe were, of the thin layer of water seeping up over the edge of the ice.

"Easy, Ironheart," David warned again.

Ironheart stopped and looked around.

"Hike! Hike!" David shouted.

Ironheart leaned his powerful chest into the

51

harness and led the team toward the bank of the river.

"If anything happens—" David started to say.

At that moment Frank heard a sound like a gunshot. He looked down and saw a crack widening in the ice, inches from the right runner of the sled. The dogs had made it safely to solid ice near the bank, but the weight of the sled was too much for the thin ice in the center of the river.

"David, what do we do?" Frank shouted, pushing himself up into a crouch. "Bail out?"

"No!" David shouted back. "Hang on!"

Another, louder crack echoed in the frigid air. David jumped onto the ice and grabbed the railing of the sled, trying to hold it steady.

It was no use. Frank felt the sled tilt to the right. Before he and Joe could escape, it tipped and slid down toward the dark, freezing river.

6 Who Has the Right of Way?

When he felt the sled lurch sideways, Joe was getting to his feet. He flung his arms out to each side, trying to keep his balance, but it was no use. The railing of the sled caught him at ankle level, and he fell backward. All the breath in his lungs exploded with a loud gasp as the ice-cold water closed around him.

In shock, he scrambled frantically to reach the surface. Claustrophobic visions of drowning while trapped under the ice flashed through his mind. His boots touched bottom. He pushed upward, leading with his hands, and found himself on his feet in the middle of an ice-free patch

53

of river ten feet across. The water came halfway up his chest.

"Frank! David!" he choked out. "Help!"

"Hold on, Joe!" Frank shouted back. "We'll get you out of there!"

Joe could feel the icy water draining away his precious body heat. He had to get out of the water as fast as he could, but he also knew he had to remain calm. Struggling and thrashing around in panic would only sap his strength faster.

He began to wade toward the edge of the river, but his boots kept skidding on the bottom. Finally he stopped and stood in one place. He was afraid that if he let himself slip underwater a second time, he wouldn't be able to make it back to the surface. The freezing water felt like thousands of needles jabbing into his skin.

Thanks to the dog team, the sled had not fallen into the water. David and Frank were rummaging through it. What were they after? Couldn't they see this was an emergency? Then David stood up with a hatchet in his hand and sprinted toward the woods.

"Hey, where's he going? I'm freezing to death!" Joe shouted.

"Hold on!" Frank answered. "David's getting something to help us reach you."

"H-h-hurry," Joe pleaded, through chattering teeth. "I can't feel my feet and legs."

54

Frank got down on his hands and knees and crawled across the ice toward Joe. He had gone only a few feet when Joe heard an ominous popping sound.

"No, Frank!" Joe shouted. "Go back! The ice won't hold your weight!"

"I'm not going to leave you there to turn into a human icicle," Frank said.

"It won't do me any good if you fall in, too," Joe pointed out. "Wait for David. He knows about this stuff."

Reluctance was written all over Frank's face, but he gingerly backed away from the edge of the ice. A few moments later David came running out of the woods with a long birch branch in his hand.

"Frank," he said, "lie down with your feet on the bank and get a good hold on my ankles."

"What are you going to do?" Frank demanded.

"The trick with thin ice is to spread out your weight," David explained. He lay flat and began inching across the ice toward Joe, pushing the branch in front of himself. "Can you reach it, Joe?"

Joe stretched his right arm as far as he could. The end of the branch was only inches away from his fingertips, but it might as well have been miles. "I can't!" he shouted back, trying to keep the desperation he was feeling out of his voice.

David moved forward, this time dangerously close to the line where ice and water met. "Now?"

Joe reached again but still not far enough.

"Come on, Joe!" Frank was still hanging on to David's ankles. "You can do it."

Joe took a deep breath. He felt his strength draining away.

David pushed the branch out another two inches. "One more time," he said.

Joe focused his attention on the branch. Then, with all the strength he had left, he lunged forward. He felt his fingers close on the end of the branch and his feet slip out from under him. He was immersed in the freezing water again, but this time he was too numb to feel cold.

"You did it!" Frank cheered.

"Other hand!" David called. "You can do it."

Joe took a deep breath and scrambled to his feet on the slick river bottom to force himself closer to the branch. He was sure he was going to lose the grip he had, but he managed to bring both hands together on the branch.

"Great! Now, just hang on!" David said. He began to inch backward, towing the branch and Joe after him. Frank helped by pulling on David's ankles. After a few moments that felt like forever, Joe found himself lying on solid ice.

Frank cheered and slapped Joe on his back, but

David said, "No time to lose." He ordered Iron-heart to stay where he was, then told Joe and Frank to follow him onto solid ground.

"He needs a blanket," Frank said.

Joe stood shivering, his body huddled against the severe cold.

"No," David said. "First thing, he has to get out of his wet clothes."

"Here?" Frank asked. "Now?"

"They'll suck the warmth and the life out of him if he leaves them on," David continued. "You'll find an emergency kit in the sled. There's a space blanket in it. Get him out of his clothes and wrap the blanket around him. I'm going for kindling."

Joe's fingers were too numb to manage a zipper or button. Frank helped him undress, then wrapped the ultrathin metallic blanket around him.

Joe controlled the chattering of his teeth long enough to say, "Do you think this'll make me a life member of the Polar Bear Club?"

"Count on it," Frank replied, patting his shoulder. "They'll probably name you honorary president!"

David returned, carrying a double handful of brown tangled grass. He cleared the snow away from a flat place and put the grass in a little heap.

"What is that?" Frank asked.

"A field mouse nest," David said. He stacked dry twigs over the mouse nest, then took a wooden match from a waterproof holder, struck the match against the scratchy side of the holder, and ignited the nest.

Once the tinder was lit, he added larger twigs, then thin sticks, then larger branches. Soon he had a blazing fire. The three huddled close to it, soaking in the lifesaving warmth. When Joe finally looked up and smiled for the first time, so did Frank and David.

While Joe's clothes dried in front of the fire, the young men ate dried peaches and hardtack crackers from the emergency kit. David melted some snow and brewed up a can of spruce-needle tea to wash down the snack. Finally they felt ready to hit the trail back to Glitter. They put out the fire, turned the sled around, and got the dog team ready again.

"I think we've had enough training for one day," David said with a grin.

"Enough for two or three days," Joe retorted.

"More like two or three months," Frank said.

They mushed back the way they had come and reached the Yukon. Ironheart led the way along the trail down the middle of the river.

A little later David said, "I know, I see him."

"What?" Frank asked.

"I was talking to Ironheart," David explained. "There's a team coming in our direction. He spotted it before I did."

"How'd you know that?" Joe asked.

"You get to know the details up here," David said. "Little signs."

"I can't see a thing," Frank said. "Just a whole lot of ice and sky."

Ironheart kept a steady pace for the rest of the dogs, but he held his head high to keep an eye on the other team ahead.

"Is the other team on this trail?" Joe asked.

David nodded. "Yes, it's Gregg."

"You can recognize him at this distance?" Joe asked, amazed. "All I can see is a black dot on the ice!"

"Out here in the bush, you get to know how to figure things out from a distance. If you don't, you're in trouble," David said. "I can tell you how big his team is, how fast he's moving, and how good a musher he is from the shapes they make against the sky."

"What's Gregg doing out here?" Frank asked.

David shrugged. "He's training."

"I wish he'd do it somewhere else," Joe said. "I don't feel like meeting anybody right now."

The two dog teams closed the distance between them. One glance told Joe that the trail was only wide enough for a single team.

"David?" he called. "Who has the right of way?"

"That's not how we think out here," David replied.

"I'll bet that's how Gregg thinks," Frank said.

By the time the two teams were fifty yards apart, it was clear Gregg wasn't going to slow down.

David pressed the brake into the ice-packed trail and commanded Ironheart to stop. Joe and Frank jumped out of the sled and helped him move it to the side of the trail. Then David pulled Ironheart and the other dogs out of the way and ordered them to be still.

Gregg mushed straight toward them without slowing down or greeting them.

"What'd I tell you?" Frank said.

David said nothing, but Joe knew he wasn't going to risk a dog fight between the two teams. Gregg could show how big and tough he was by pressing for the right of way, but David was more concerned about keeping his dogs in shape for the Iditarod.

When Gregg was about a dozen feet away, David held up his hand, signaling him to stop. Staring straight ahead, Gregg ignored him. With an icy *whoosh*, the dogsled sped past and disappeared into the distance.

"That guy has a major attitude problem," Joe said.

"I wanted to warn him about the thin ice," David said. He sounded sad.

"A cold bath would probably do him good," Frank said. "It doesn't seem to have hurt Joe."

"Very funny," said Joe. "Come on, let's get back to the cabin. My clothes are still damp."

As soon as Glitter came into sight, the dogs picked up speed. Their tails started wagging, and a new energy showed in their powerful steps.

Ironheart led them up the riverbank and onto the trail to their kennel. After David unharnessed the team, with help from Joe and Frank, and checked their food and water, the three started down the path toward David's family's cabin.

They were nearly there when Joe said, "Look, isn't that Justine?"

"She looks upset about something," David said.

Justine ran up the path toward them.

"David," she called while she was still a few yards away. "Come quick! My dad's sick."

"Peter?" Joe asked.

She nodded.

61

"What is it? What happened?" David demanded.

"I don't know. It was something he ate that made him really, really sick." Justine's eyes filled with tears. "David, I'm so scared. I'm afraid he's dying!"

7 Driving the Point Deep

David stood paralyzed with shock. Then he whirled and dashed toward his cabin with Frank and Joe close behind. They burst through the door and stopped dead.

Peter was lying on the bed, doubled up and groaning. His hands clutched at his stomach. Mona sat beside him, wiping his forehead with a damp cloth.

David went over and put his hand on Mona's shoulder. "What happened?" he asked. "What is it?"

"I don't know," Mona answered. "All of a sudden he had this terrible pain. He barely made it to the bed."

"I'm so worried," Justine said, looking at Frank and Joe. "We have to do something."

Mona stood up. "David?" she said. "I can't leave Peter like this. Will you go to the grove for me? You know what to look for."

David hurried toward the door. "You come, too," he said to Frank and Joe. "You can help."

"Where are we going?" Frank asked as he and Joe followed David along a trail into the forest.

"The grove," David said. "It's a place that Mona knows about."

"What's there?" Joe asked.

"Mona's a healer," David replied. "Her mother and grandmother were, too. To help Peter, she needs some plants and roots that grow only in the grove."

Frank had heard about Native American healers. Like peoples in other areas, David's people had learned over hundreds of years which local herbs, leaves, and roots were helpful in treating illnesses. Even the big drug companies had learned to respect this knowledge. Teams of scientists were traveling to all parts of the world to find out as much as they could before the ancient lores were lost.

After a twenty-minute hike Frank noticed a change in the trees. The dense stand of spruce was behind them, and they were in an open area of mixed birches and aspens. The bare, ice-decked branches sparkled in the weak sunlight.

"Over there," David said, pointing to a patch of ground near the base of a big oak. "Brush the snow away and dig up some of the moss you'll find growing there."

Frank and Joe ran to the spot and worked together, exposing and gathering thick, earthy-smelling moss. Meanwhile, David dug up a patch of low-growing wintergreen, cut a section of bark off a black cherry birch, sliced off root sections of an alder bush, and took twigs from other trees and shrubs Frank didn't recognize.

Ten minutes later the three friends were on their way back to Glitter. The return hike went faster. When they got to the cabin, they found it filled with a strange aroma. On the stove a black iron kettle bubbled and steamed. Mona stood near it, putting in handfuls of herbs. She took the bag of stuff that David and the Hardys had collected and started adding that, too.

While the herbal remedy steeped, Frank asked Mona, "Do you know what made Peter sick?"

She shook her head. "Maybe the apple he ate was bad," she said. "He started feeling sick right afterward."

"Did you or Justine eat any of it?" asked Joe.

"Just him," Mona said.

David said, "I didn't know we had any apples."

"We didn't," Justine told him. "It was a present from Curt Stone. We got a whole basket of fresh fruit from him."

Frank looked over at Joe and saw that his thoughts were running along the same lines. Why would Curt send a present to Peter? He had to know that Peter was one of the leaders of the opposition to ThemeLife's plans for Glitter. Was the basket of fruit meant as a bribe? A pretty stingy one, if so.

But what if Curt had deliberately poisoned one of the apples? Frank wondered. It sounded like something out of a fairy tale, but such things were known to happen. If Peter or one of his family got sick, it would keep Peter from organizing the town against the theme park. In fact, this and the fire in Peter's cabin and the damage to Ralph Hunter's boat could *all* be part of a plot to scare off people who were opposed to ThemeLife!

"Where'd Curt get fresh fruit at this time of year?" David asked.

Mona looked up from stirring the caldron. "It must have come in on the bush plane," she said. "We thought he gave it to us to help us feel better about losing our cabin."

"What did he say when he brought it?" Joe asked.

"He didn't bring it," Mona replied.

"Gregg brought it," Justine added.

"Hold it, I'm a little confused," Frank said. "Why did Gregg bring it?"

Justine said, "Jake asked him to."

Mona must have seen the look of confusion on Frank's face. She said, "Flip Atkins, the bush pilot, flies in the mail deliveries and food orders from Fairbanks. Everything but the mail goes to Jake at the general store. Then he delivers any special orders. Or asks somebody like Gregg to do it for him."

Frank opened his mouth to ask another question, but Mona held up her hand to stop him. She pulled on a pair of thick gloves and lifted the hot kettle. Justine held a piece of cloth over the mouth of an earthenware pot, and Mona poured the steamy liquid from the plants into the pot, straining it through the cloth.

She then scooped a ladleful of the brew into a thick mug, poured in a little spring water to cool it, stirred in a teaspoon of honey, and took it over to Peter. Justine helped her father sit up on the edge of the bed while Mona held the mug to his lips.

Peter finished drinking and lay down again. Frank asked Mona, "This basket of fruit—was there a card with it?"

Mona crossed the room to the dresser and

67

returned with a business card in her hand. Frank and Joe looked at it. It read, Curt Stone, Field Representative, ThemeLife, Inc. Handwritten on the back were the words "Best wishes, Curt."

"That's his card, all right," Frank said. "But it doesn't have *your* names on it anywhere. He could have given that card to someone else, who put it in that basket of fruit. Someone like Gregg, for instance."

"I don't get it," David said. "Are you saying there was something wrong with the fruit?"

"There's no way to tell without a lab test," Joe said. "But after what happened to Peter, I don't think *I'm* going to try to eat any of that fruit."

David's face reddened. "If Gregg thinks he can force me to drop out of the Iditarod by making me and my family sick, he's going to find out different. And after I've beat him in the race, I'm going to do some major alterations on his face!"

Justine put her hand on his arm. "David, we don't know that Gregg did anything wrong," she said. "I know you and he don't get along, but he's always been nice to me. I don't think he'd try to hurt us."

Mona looked from Joe to Frank and said, "I hope you can get to the bottom of this, before anything worse happens."

She took the mug from the table and went back

to Peter's side. "How are you feeling?" she asked.

"Better," he croaked.

"Good. Want some more?" she said, holding up the mug.

Peter scrunched up his face. "That horrible stuff? Eeyuukk."

"It's good," Mona said, smiling. "It worked on you, didn't it?"

"Maybe it's good for my stomach," Peter replied. "But it's eeyuukk for my mouth."

He tried to sit up. Mona pressed his shoulders back down. "Rest," she said. "You need it."

"See what happens when you take something from ThemeLife?" Peter said, lying back. "Next thing you know, you're sick as a dog."

"Hey, watch how you talk about dogs," David said. "The Iditarod's just a few days away!"

Just after nightfall Mona said she wanted to fix Peter some good, healthy moose steak. "Would somebody like to get some from the cache?" she asked, smiling and looking at Frank and Joe.

"Sure," Joe said, leaping to his feet.

"Where is it?" Frank asked.

"In the shed behind our cabin," Mona said. "There's most of a side of moose hanging there. You'll find a big knife and a saw, too."

69

"How much do you want?" Frank asked as he donned his parka.

Mona held her hands out, about six inches apart. "About this much," she said.

David lit a lantern for them, and the Hardys set off into the darkness. The Arctic sky was thickly sprinkled with glittering stars. An owl hooted nearby, and a small animal scurried away through the bushes.

"They just leave their meat supply outside in a shed?" Joe asked.

Frank laughed. "Don't worry, it won't spoil. The whole outdoors is one big freezer compartment."

"I get it," Joe said. "Now I see why Mona mentioned that saw. We're going to need it to cut off the meat."

The Windman cabin still smelled of smoke. Frank and Joe went around it and found the shed. Joe pulled open the door, and they stepped inside.

Frank held up the lantern and looked around. To the left, fur pelts were stacked, stiff and frozen, on a wooden crate. A two-man crosscut saw hung from a spike on the back wall. Other tools lay tossed in a big woven basket.

"So where's the moose?" Joe wondered, peering around. "Do you suppose Mona sent us out here as a joke or something?"

70

"I don't think so," Frank said. "She needs that meat for dinner."

"Fine," Joe said. "But where is it?"

Frank held the lantern higher. "There's a big hook in that beam," he said. "It looks like that's where the side of meat *ought* to be hanging. The only problem is, it isn't."

"Frank," Joe said, in a changed voice. "Frank, look!"

Frank turned and looked. Painted on the plank wall with black paint was the rough outline of a heart. But this was no Valentine card. Protruding from the center of the heart was a wicked-looking butcher knife, the point driven deep into the wood.

8 News Travels Fast

Joe and Frank stared at the knife stuck in the wall. After a long moment of silence Joe said, "The Windmans are counting on that meat to last them until spring, aren't they?"

Frank nodded grimly. "Probably."

"What kind of rat would steal a family's food?" Joe asked.

"A two-legged rat," Frank said. "But I don't think he cares about the meat. He wants to frighten Peter and Mona by showing them how easily they can be hurt."

Frank went over to the wall, put his nose near the painted heart, and sniffed. "The paint's fresh," he reported. "At a guess, no more than a couple of hours old, unless the cold keeps it from drying."

Joe thought about that for a few seconds before saying, "We know someone who was over this way at about the right time: Gregg. What if he brought that poisoned fruit, then took the moose carcass?"

"He could have done it," Frank agreed. "But so could almost anybody. The woods are just a few steps away. You slip in, do your dirty work, and slip away."

"'Slip away'? How much do you suppose a moose weighs?" Joe asked. "They're awfully big, aren't they? You're not going to toss it over your shoulder and stroll off through town."

"That's a good point, Joe. Okay, we're not talking about a whole live moose, which might weigh as much as a ton. Let's say it's a half or maybe a quarter of a dressed carcass. And Peter and Mona have been living off it since fall. Even so, what's left must weigh a hundred pounds or more—maybe a lot more! Here, let's take a look around outside. But watch where you step."

Even by the flickering light of the kerosene lantern, the tracks were easy to spot: two ruts about an inch wide, the distance between them about a foot and a half.

"That's too narrow for a dogsled," Joe pointed out.

"Remember when Justine went to get water from the spring?" Frank asked. "She used a sledge she pulled by hand."

Joe felt his jaw drop in shock. "Justine! Frank, you're not saying——"

"Of course not," Frank said quickly. "But what do you want to bet she left the sledge outside the cabin, where anyone could get it?"

Joe knelt down in the snow to get a closer look at the marks left by the sledge. "Look, Frank!" he said. "The tracks get deeper off to the left. The thief must have pushed or pulled it here from the path, loaded the meat on it, then gone off in the direction of the woods."

From the darkness David's voice called, "Joe? Frank?"

"Over here, David," Joe called back.

When David joined them, the Hardys quickly explained what they had found—and *not* found—inside the shed. David muttered a string of words in Athabascan. Joe didn't understand a single one, but he was sure they weren't compliments.

"We found the tracks of a sledge," Frank told him, and held the lantern near the marks.

To Joe's surprise, David got down on his hands and knees and put his face close to the tracks and felt the snow. When he stood up, he said, "This was Uncle Peter's sledge. And the theft was just after sunset."

"How can you tell?" Frank asked.

"From the way the snow looks and feels on the bottom and sides of the track," David told him. "Let's find out where the thief went."

As Joe had suspected, the trail led into the woods. They hadn't followed it more than fifty yards when David held up a hand and said, "Wait—there's something in the bushes on the left."

Frank held the lantern up at arm's length. Joe narrowed his eyes and stared in the direction David had indicated, but he couldn't make out anything more than a dark shape.

David laughed aloud. "It's our moose meat!" he said. "The thief must have dropped it here. We'll have dinner after all!"

They carried the frozen carcass back to the shed. While Joe and Frank sawed off a roast-size piece for dinner, David went back to follow the trail of the thief. A few minutes later he returned with the news that the thief had pulled the sledge around to the front of the cabin and left it there.

"I told Joe I thought the thief wasn't after the meat at all," Frank said as they walked back to the cabin.

75

David nodded. "What he wanted was to cause trouble for us. First he set our cabin on fire, then he threw the log through the window, then he doctored the fruit that made Uncle Peter sick, and now this. Somebody must hate us very much."

Joe was tempted to say that the incidents could have occurred for business reasons, not personal ones. He kept quiet. A business motive would probably upset David even more than the thought of having a personal enemy.

The next morning, while David was taking care of his huskies, Frank and Joe went into town to pursue their investigation. The first person they ran across was Curt Stone.

"Hi, boys," Curt said when he saw them. "How are you enjoying your stay?"

"Fine," Frank said. "Say, can we ask you about that basket of fruit?"

"Ask away," Curt replied. "What basket of fruit?"

"The one you sent to Peter and Mona yesterday," Joe told him.

"Nope, not me," Curt said easily. "Though, now you mention it, I *should* do something to show my sympathy, with all the trouble they're having. I heard someone tried to steal their meat cache last night. Terrible, the things that happen."

"How did you hear about that?" Frank asked.

Curt shrugged. "I told you. News travels fast in a little place like this," he said. "But what's this about a basket of fruit?"

"Peter and Mona got a basket of fresh fruit yesterday, with your card in it," Frank explained. He studied Curt's face, which didn't change, then went on. "Peter got sick after eating one of the apples."

Curt gave him a hard look. "I don't like what you're hinting at," he said. "I didn't send any fruit to anyone yesterday."

"What about your card?" Joe asked.

"Half the population of Glitter must have my business card by now," Curt retorted. "That's what I print them up for—to give out to people."

Before either of the Hardys could think of a comeback to this, Curt added, "You boys will have to excuse me. I've got matters to attend to that are a lot more important than your wild accusations."

He walked away.

After a moment Frank said, "*Somebody* sent that basket of fruit."

"We know who delivered it," Joe pointed out. "Somebody who has a grudge against David. Maybe it carries over to David's relatives."

"Let's see what Jake has to say about it," Frank suggested. "And while we're there, I'd like to use Jake's two-way radio to put in a call to Dad. He can look into the ThemeLife company for us."

"Great idea!" Joe said.

Fenton Hardy, Frank and Joe's father, had retired years before from the New York City police department to become a leading private investigator.

When Frank told Jake what they wanted, he led them to the back room and radioed Fairbanks. A minute later the link to Bayport went through. Jake handed the telephone receiver to Frank.

Frank took it and waited with his palm over the microphone.

Jake got the hint. "I'll give you some privacy," he said, and left the room.

Frank and Joe took turns telling their father about Glitter and their dogsledding adventures on the Yukon River. They didn't mention the fire or the other strange incidents. Anyone with a short wave set could be listening in on their call.

At the end of the call Frank said, "Oh, and there's a big campaign here by a company called ThemeLife to set up a theme park in the area. We'd sure like to know more about the company. It sounds very interesting—very. You don't know anything about it, do you? ThemeLife?"

"Why, no," Mr. Hardy replied. "But if you fellows think it's interesting, I'm sure it is. Maybe I'll ask around about it. I'm sure your mom and Aunt Gertrude would like to say hello, but they're out shopping. Can you arrange to be at this number one hour from now?"

Frank gave a sigh of relief. His father had understood. "No problem, Dad," he said. "We'll make a point of it."

After Frank hung up, he said softly to Joe, "He'll look into it and call back in an hour. We'd better wait before we ask Jake about the fruit."

"Until after we've heard from Dad, you mean?" Joe replied. "Right—or else something might go wrong with Jake's radio."

Frank and Joe spent the next forty-five minutes trying to find Gregg. Several people said they had seen him that morning, but Frank and Joe never managed to catch up to him. They'd have to question him later. It was time to go back to Jake's store for the call from their father.

Frank took the call, which lasted less than a minute, during which he wrote down what he was hearing. When he got off, he showed Joe his notes, which read, "Sound reputation but desperate financial situation. Success of new projects crucial to company survival."

"I think we're onto something here," Frank said in an undertone.

" 'Survival,' " Joe quoted. "That's a pretty powerful motive to do whatever it takes to swing the vote your way. Even if it means trying to poison your opponents."

Frank glanced at the open doorway, then murmured, "Curt says he never sent that basket."

"He would, wouldn't he?" Joe responded. "Let's find out what Jake can tell us about it."

They went into the main room. Jake was behind the polished oak counter, making a pyramid of condensed milk cans. He looked up and said, "Your call go through all right, boys?"

"Yes, thanks," Frank replied. "Oh, Jake? Did you send a basket of fruit to Peter yesterday?"

The storekeeper shook his head. "Nope. Curt Stone sent it. All I did was ask Gregg to carry it over. Why?"

"That's funny," Joe said. "We saw Curt earlier, and he said he didn't know anything about that fruit."

Jake's face reddened. "He sent it, all right. I found it right here on my counter, with his card and a note saying to send it to Peter."

Frank asked, "Do you mean that you didn't speak to him about it, just found the note?" Jake nodded. "Do you still have it?"

"Nope," Jake said. "Say, what is this? Is Curt up to something? If he is, I bet Lucky's in it, too, up to his neck."

"The prospector?" Joe asked. "Why?"

Jake looked down at the counter. "I'm no tattletale," he said, with a little smile. "But yesterday when I glanced out my window, I saw Curt passing Lucky a wad of bills. He looked as if he didn't want anybody to see it, either. The way I figure it, Lucky must be doing something to earn that money. Am I right?"

Frank and Joe thanked Jake for his help and left the store. Once on the street Frank said, "We'd better have a talk with Lucky."

They stopped by the cabin to get directions, then hiked into the hills behind town. Lucky's mining operation was a twenty-minute walk from Glitter, on a dirt road that looked like a relic from Gold Rush days.

Frank was first to spot the weathered shack beside a frozen stream. "Hello, Lucky?" he called.

No answer. He walked nearer and called again.

From behind him he heard a faint footstep. He started to turn, but an arm caught him around the throat and started to tighten, cutting off his breath.

81

9 More Dirty Tricks

Joe was out back, trying to figure out a complicated piece of old machinery he'd spotted. He heard a strangled shout and looked up and recognized Lucky's dirty green parka and faded red cap. Lucky had his arm in a choke hold around Frank's neck.

Not for long. As Joe rushed to help his brother, Frank got grips on Lucky's wrist and elbow, then made a sudden leap to the side. An instant later he had a hammerlock on his astonished attacker.

"Let go, you're hurting me!" Lucky protested. "I'm an old man!"

"You should have thought of that before you jumped me," Frank retorted. He released

Lucky's arm and took two quick steps backward, ready to meet any further attack.

Lucky scowled and rubbed the muscle of his upper arm. "You were spying on me, that's what," he said. "I can't stand spies."

"We just wanted to talk to you," Joe said. "We didn't mean to scare you." The instant he said it, he realized that he had used the wrong word.

"Scare me!" Lucky said. "You think you scared me? *Nobody* scares me!"

"No, no," Joe said hastily. "What I meant to say is that we didn't mean to surprise you."

Lucky spat on the ground. "You didn't surprise me neither," he growled. "You don't creep up on Lucky Moeller. I saw you coming. I heard you coming. I even *smelled* you coming!"

"Well," Frank said. "Now that we're here, can we talk?"

Lucky peered at them from under his bushy eyebrows. "What about?" he asked, suspicious.

"We were wondering what you think about the ThemeLife plan," Joe said. "How do you think people in Glitter ought to vote?"

Lucky's face brightened. "You boys doing a survey? Well, I think everybody ought to vote yes. Why wouldn't they?"

"What do you think is good about the ThemeLife plan?" asked Frank.

Lucky's head bobbed up and down as he said, "The money, that's what. The money! All those tourists coming to town with their pockets stuffed with money. Hundreds of them, thousands of them. And they'll all come out here to tour my mine. It'll be the biggest attraction around—the Gold Rush days live again. In a year or two I'll make enough to retire to Florida."

Lucky reached deep into his pants pocket and brought out a clenched fist. Stretching it out toward Joe and Frank, he said, "See this?"

They looked down at his rough, dirty hand. "What?" Frank asked.

Lucky opened his hand. A gold nugget the size of a bean gleamed in the weak sunlight.

"Wow!" Joe exclaimed.

Lucky smiled, revealing the stub of a front tooth.

"You found that here?" Frank asked.

"Sure I did," Lucky replied. He turned and walked quickly toward the frozen creek, talking a mile a minute as he went. Frank and Joe had to hurry to stay up with him.

"I found this one thirty years ago," he said, holding up the fist with the gold nugget. "Found it in the creek. This creek's evil and cunning, but I'm smarter than it is. For thousands of years now, it's been washing gold out of the hillsides and carrying it down by here. It means to dump it in the Yukon, so it's lost forever. But as soon as it gets this far, *I* take it and I keep it!"

"Do you pan for it?" Frank asked him.

Joe remembered seeing pictures of gold miners, squatting beside streams with large, shallow pans in their hands. They'd fill the pans with gravel and creek water, then slowly swirl the sand and water out. Gold was heavier than rock, so it would sink to the bottom of the pan.

"Panning? Panning's for fools," Lucky said scornfully. "I run a placer mine."

He pointed toward a long wooden trough that ran from farther up the creek to just next to his shack. "See that? Come summer, I dig up the gravel from the streambed and put it in there. The water washes it down the chute, and the gold drops into the box because it's so heavy. Then I go and collect the dust and specks and nuggets, and stash them away."

"Do you find a lot of gold that way?" Joe asked.

"I'm not saying," Lucky replied, giving them a shrewd look. "But I'll tell you one thing. You want gold these days, you don't go looking for it in the hills. You got to work too hard for it that way. The real gold is in tourists' pockets."

Frank laughed. "You sound like you ought to be on the payroll of the ThemeLife Company," he said.

"They haven't asked me," Lucky replied.

Joe broke in to say, "Haven't they? We heard that you were working for Curt Stone. Somebody saw him giving you a lot of money."

Lucky spun around to face him, his fists clenched. "Who said that?" he demanded.

"Jake Ferguson," Joe told him.

"Jake lies like a dog!" Lucky shouted, swinging his arms around like a windmill. "There's bad blood between us, and it's all his doing. From the day he figured out that I'm not going to let him cheat me the way he does everyone else, he's been after me. As for Curt Stone, he never gave me anything but the time of day, and that's flat."

Frank opened his mouth to ask another question, but Lucky went on, "Get off my claim, both of you, and don't let me see you around here again. I was right to start with. You're a couple of spies, that's what you are!"

Joe looked over at Frank and motioned with his head. They weren't going to get any more information out of Lucky. They turned and started back down the trail to town.

Once they were out of Lucky's hearing, Frank said, "Well, somebody's lying. But who? Lucky? Why would he want to keep us from finding out that he's working for Curt—unless he's doing more than just talking to people?"

Joe was about to reply when he heard a sound in the distance that made the hairs on the back of his neck stand up. "Frank!" he said. "That was a wolf howl!"

Frank grinned at him. "It sure sounded like it," he replied. "Unless it was Lucky, trying to make us nervous."

"Well, if it was, he succeeded," Joe said glumly. "How far are we from town?"

"Why? Do you think the wolves know that they're not allowed inside the city limits?" Frank joked.

"Very funny," Joe said, glancing over his shoulder. In every direction the woods were silent, dark, and deep. The slinking shapes he sensed in the shadows were just his imagination, he hoped.

"Or it could be Jake who's lying," Frank said, picking up the thread of the conversation. "He may be out to make trouble for Lucky."

As the Hardys walked briskly down the last slope before the town, Joe spotted Curt coming out of a cabin on the outskirts of town. "I bet he's out canvassing for votes," he said. "One thing you have to say, he's a hard worker. Let's ask him about Lucky."

Curt saw them coming and waited for them to catch up. "Out taking a tour of the area?" he asked.

"We went up to see Lucky Moeller's placer mine," Frank told him.

"Good for you," Curt said with a smile. "It's one of the real landmarks of the area. Of course, you probably had some trouble figuring out exactly what goes on there. It's not set up for visitors yet. But once it is, I guarantee it'll be a high point of Historic Glitter, Gold Rush Town."

Joe said, "Lucky seemed pretty enthusiastic about your project."

Curt nodded. "He should be. It'll make him a star. You're not going to find a more typical old-time prospector, even in Hollywood. I wouldn't be surprised if he ends up with the biggest salary on the ThemeLife payroll. Bigger even than the project director."

"I thought he was already on the ThemeLife payroll," Frank said in a casual voice.

Curt gave him a sharp look. "Where'd you hear that?" he demanded.

"I don't know—around," Frank said with a shrug. "Why? Isn't he?"

"I'm the only full-time employee of the ThemeLife Company in Glitter," Curt said. "Anyone who says different doesn't know what he's talking about. I'd better run along. There are still a few people who don't understand all the advantages our project will bring to their town."

He turned and hurried away.

"Interesting," Frank said. "Did you notice? He said he's the only *full-time* ThemeLife employee here. He could still be paying Lucky to help talk people around. . . ."

"Or to play dirty tricks on them if they won't be talked around," Joe said. "We'd better keep a close eye on Mr. Curt Stone."

David's kennel was around the next bend of the trail. The huskies were barking and straining at their tethers.

"Do you suppose they're saying hello to us?" Joe wondered aloud. He called, "Hi, doggies!"

"Joe, look," Frank said. "One of them got away!"

The short end of a rope dangled limply from one of the sturdy stakes that kept the huskies near their houses. "Must have chewed through the rope," Joe said.

David came running up the path. When he saw the dangling rope, his face turned pale. "Big Foot, gone?" He groaned. "Oh, no!"

He went from one dog to the next, speaking softly and calming them down. Joe and Frank followed his lead. Once the team was quiet, David said, "This is terrible. Big Foot is Ironheart's backup. He's the second most important member of the team. I should have come out right away, the minute I heard that wolf pack howling."

"We heard them, too," Joe said.

"They're trying to lure my huskies away to join

their pack," David explained. "It's like *The Call of the Wild.*" He went around to the dogs again, speaking softly to each one.

Frank went over to Big Foot's stake and picked up the rope. Then he looked over at Joe and gestured with his head.

Joe looked at the rope. "Hey," he said in a low voice, "the fibers are smooth and even."

"You've got it," Frank said. "Someone cut the rope almost all the way through. One good pull from Big Foot, and it snapped."

At the sound of another distant howl, David's team erupted into barking again. "Easy, easy," David said.

"You calm them down," Frank said. "Joe and I'll go look for Big Foot."

"Wait," David called, but Joe and Frank were already following Big Foot's pawprints into the woods.

"Now I know why he's called Big Foot," Joe said. "Good thing the snow isn't too hard."

"Or too deep," Frank replied. "Am I right that David's dogs started barking just before we got there?"

Joe thought for a moment. "I think so."

"Then there's a good chance that was when Big Foot broke his rope and headed for the tall timber," Frank said. "If so, he probably hasn't gone far."

Frank and Joe followed Big Foot's trail across a clearing into the woods.

Another long series of slow, high-pitched howls came floating through the woods. Frank and Joe paused in midstride and looked at each other.

"That sounds a lot closer," Joe said, lowering his voice.

Frank cleared his throat and said, "Good. Maybe Big Foot's close, too."

The tracks led to a small clearing. When they stepped out from the trees, the howls stopped.

Frank and Joe froze. The sudden stillness was eerie.

A gray-brown wolf the size of a large dog padded out from under the trees and stopped. Then three more appeared. Tails twitching, the four wolves stood side by side and calmly looked across the clearing at Joe and Frank.

10 A Circle of Wolves

The four wolves stood like statues, tongues lolling from the sides of their mouths. Frank found himself wondering if they were laughing at the expressions on the faces of their prey. The only other movement was a slight twitching of their tails.

"Any ideas, Frank?" Joe muttered out of the side of his mouth.

"Tell them we come in peace and ask them to take us to their leader," Frank muttered back.

"Thanks a bunch," Joe said. "Any *good* ideas?"

Frank shrugged. "No sudden moves. We don't

want them to get the idea that we're about to attack them. *Or* that we're afraid of them."

"I'll try to keep that in mind," Joe retorted.

"Let's see what happens if we back off," Frank suggested. "Slowly."

Together, the two brothers took a cautious step backward, then another. As if they'd been choreographed, the wolves began to move in the same instant. Two peeled off to the left and two to the right.

"Are they giving up?" Joe asked.

"In your dreams," Frank said. "They're starting to circle us. That means they've gone over to wolf pack attack mode."

"Oh," said Joe. "I'm so glad you have a name for it."

Even though he was aware of the peril of their situation, Frank had room left over to study the wolves. They were a little bigger than huskies, and it was clear they were related to them. But the wolves were skinny, almost gaunt. Frank found himself remembering a line from the Shakespeare play *Julius Caesar* about somebody with a "lean and hungry look." The wolves had that, all right.

Where had he heard that the jaws of a wolf were twice as powerful as those of a German shepherd? Some nature show on public TV, prob-

93

ably. That was one fact he'd rather take on faith than put to the test.

"I don't believe it," Joe said. "You're right. They're trying to trap us with a pincer movement!" He took a step back.

"We can't let that happen," Frank said.

"Yeah, but how do we stop it?" Joe asked.

They were nearly out of the clearing now. Would they be safer in the woods? Or in worse trouble? Whichever it was, Frank knew that they had no choice. They had to try to reach the safety of town. Their only hope was help from other people.

Or was it?

"Joe, look!" Frank exclaimed, and grabbed his brother's arm.

From the woods to their right, a sturdy husky came trotting out into the clearing.

"That must be Big Foot," said Frank.

"I can't see his feet," Joe said, "and I don't care who it is. I hope he's on our side."

The dog stopped, faced the four circling wolves, and let out a low, menacing growl. The wolves stopped where they were and turned to look over the new actor in the show.

"Now's our chance," Frank said hastily. "Keep backing up. The second we're under the trees, run for your life!"

A few moments later their boots were shattering the crust of the snow as they ran. With each breath he took, Frank felt as if Old Man Winter were stabbing him in the chest with an icicle. He'd heard stories of people freezing their lungs by breathing too deeply in weather like this. He'd worry about that later, once they were safe from the wolf pack.

The woods thinned out, and the Hardys found themselves on a well-traveled trail. They turned in the direction of town and kept running. Then, over a rise a few dozen yards ahead, David and his team came speeding into view. As if on signal, Frank and Joe dropped into a heap by the side of the trail and tried to catch their breaths.

David brought the dogsled to a stop and ran over to them. "Are you all right?" he asked anxiously. "What happened?"

Frank took a deep breath, swallowed, and said, "Wolves—four of them."

"They started to circle," Joe added. "But Big Foot saved us."

"He faced them down," Frank explained. "And we ran. I wish we hadn't left him there like that."

"That's what he wanted you to do," David said. "He was giving you that chance. Can you get back to town on your own? I'd better go after him. Now that the wolves know he won't join them, they may decide to attack him."

"We'll be fine. Do you think you'll be able to get him back?" Frank asked.

David looked grim. "I hope so," he said. "He's a good dog, strong and loyal. I need him for the race, in case anything happens to Ironheart."

He called to his team and pushed the sled to get it started. "Hike!" he yelled, and moments later he and the dogs vanished over a rise.

"I hope he gets Big Foot back safely," Frank said as he and Joe trotted back to town. "I wonder who cut Big Foot's tether."

"Do you think David knows the tether was cut?"

"I don't think so, but when he finds out, he's going to go ballistic. Those dogs mean everything to him."

The cabins and plank-walled shacks on the outskirts of Glitter came into view.

Frank grabbed Joe's arm. "Did you see that?" he asked urgently.

"What?" Joe asked. "Where?" Joe swiveled his head.

Frank said, "Shhh . . . There, by that shed."

A shadowy figure slipped out of a doorway that was partly open.

"That shed must hold somebody's cache," Joe said. "What's that guy doing?"

"I don't know," Frank said, studying him. "It

doesn't look right. He's up to something fishy. Come on."

They started forward, but the man saw them and set off at a run.

"Let's go!" Joe exclaimed as the man ran around the side of the cache and disappeared.

Frank followed Joe downhill to the cache and around the corner. The man was nowhere in sight.

"I don't get it," Joe said, looking around in puzzlement. "He couldn't have disappeared just like that."

Frank glanced over his shoulder. The man was slipping into the woods uphill from them. "There he goes!" Frank shouted, setting off at a run. Joe was right behind him.

Five minutes later the Hardys gave up the chase. Their quarry had too great a lead, and their escape from the wolves had used up too much of their energy.

"Pretty cute," Joe said, once he got his breathing under control. "Heading uphill like that, away from the town. I wonder what he was doing."

"Something underhanded, I bet," Frank said. "Did you get a good look at him?"

"Sure—he was wearing a green parka," Joe said. "Some help, huh? Should we check out that cache and see if we spot anything wrong?"

Frank shook his head. "Better not," he said. "We can't go poking around somebody's private property just because we saw somebody else do it. We should find out whose it is, though. Let's go ask Peter."

The only one they found at home was Justine. "Dad was feeling better so he and Mom went to the meeting," she told them. "I was just about to go there myself. Want to come?"

"What meeting?" asked Joe.

Justine looked surprised. "The whole town is getting together to talk about the ThemeLife plan. It's the last forum before the vote. Hey, do you know where David is? I know he meant to go."

"Big Foot got loose and ran away. David went after him," Frank explained.

"That's terrible," Justine said. "I hope he finds Big Foot all right. He's a very important member of David's team, and with the Iditarod just around the corner . . ."

Justine put on her parka, and the three of them walked through town to the assembly room. "Do you think he'll be here?" Joe murmured as they approached the hall.

"Who?" Frank asked.

"The guy we were chasing," Joe retorted. "Duh!"

Frank shrugged. "Will he be here?" he said. "I'd say that's a sure thing. But will we recognize him? Have you noticed how many green parkas there are in this town? Not a chance!"

The room was already crowded. They found seats in one of the back rows, just as a man Frank didn't know called the meeting to order.

"That's Reeve Anderson," Justine whispered. "Gregg's father."

Mr. Anderson explained that Curt Stone was there to answer any questions people had about the ThemeLife project and that there would be plenty of time for discussion from the floor.

Curt gave a short speech about the benefits his company's plans would bring to Glitter. Frank found his eyelids starting to droop. Then Lucky got to his feet and started to speak. Frank sat up straight, wide awake again.

"If I could make a go of mining," Lucky said, "I'd do it. And if you could make a go of hunting and fishing, you'd do it. But you know we're all about two inches from starving. These days the gold isn't in the riverbeds, it's in the tourists' pockets. But to get it into *our* pockets, first we got to get the tourists to Glitter. That's what this project is going to do, and that's why we ought to get in back of it one thousand percent!"

A lot of the audience—about half of them, by

Frank's estimate—started clapping loudly. The ones who weren't clapping looked confused and troubled.

Peter stood up. "Lucky's right," he said. Frank heard some gasps and a murmur of disbelief from around the hall. Was Peter, one of the strongest opponents of the plan, changing his mind?

"Lucky's right," Peter said again. "About one thing, at least. Our town's in trouble. We all know it. And we've got to do something about it. We all know that, too. But is Curt's project the right thing to do about it? I don't think so."

Frank heard Justine, next to him, give a deep sigh of relief.

"For hundreds of years," Peter continued, "we've lived in harmony with the land. We've hunted moose in the fall and fished for salmon in the summer. In the long winter months we've trained our dog teams and passed on our traditional crafts, which museums all over the world want to have in their collections. Do we want to give up all that for the sake of putting on a show for tourists? If we do, this won't be our town anymore. It'll be what some stranger in an office thousands of miles from here thinks our town *ought* to be. I don't think that's what we want."

Peter sat down. Again, Frank estimated that about half the audience clapped and cheered . . . the other half, this time.

From the front of the room Curt said, "Peter, I have a lot of respect for your views, and I understand your worries. But remember, the reason ThemeLife wants to come here is that you've managed to hold on to your traditional way of life. Would we do anything to interfere with that? We'd be cutting our own throats! No, I can assure you—"

Whatever he was going to assure never got assured. An explosion rocked the assembly room, sending people jumping out of their seats.

11 Explosive Confessions

"Is anyone hurt?" someone shouted.

A torrent of questions and exclamations rushed through the crowded room. "Let's get out of here!" someone else cried. A stampede headed toward the only door.

"Everybody, take it easy!" Anderson shouted from the front of the room. "Calm down! Don't push! There's no danger! The explosion was outside."

Joe and Frank pulled Justine out of the way of the panicked crowd, then linked arms with her between them to keep her from being trampled. Throughout the room levelheaded townspeople were talking to people and holding them back from joining the rush to the door. Gradually the panic died down.

Joe heard Peter shout, "Away from the door, everybody! Give people air!"

Joe looked around. Peter was standing on a chair with his hands cupped to his mouth. "Let the firefighters out first," Peter continued. "Come on, neighbors, back off!"

With sheepish looks the people around Joe and Frank inched back, leaving a path clear to the door. A dozen people Joe recognized from the bucket brigade the day before ran outside, followed by an orderly stream of others.

"Come on," Joe murmured to Frank. "Let's try for that gap in the line."

The Hardys let themselves be carried outside by the crowd. As he passed through the narrow doorway, Joe felt like a grain of sand in an hourglass, but an instant later he was outside. He took a deep breath of the cold, pure air.

Not so pure. A layer of gray smoke blanketed the town. The source was not far away, near the riverfront. It looked like—

"My store!" Jake shouted, pushing through the crowd. "My store's on fire!"

He broke into a run. Joe and Frank were close behind him. When they had closed half the distance, Frank gasped, "I don't think it's Jake's store. It's something out back."

Joe could see that Frank was right. The flames and smoke were coming from a wooden building the size of a one-car garage, about twenty feet from the rear wall of the store.

The volunteer firefighters were already hard at work, passing buckets of water and throwing them through the shattered windows. Just as the Hardys joined the crowd, they heard a crash. Flames shot up to treetop height as part of the roof fell in.

His face pale, Jake was standing in the crowd near Joe and Frank. "Well, at least it isn't the store," he said.

"What's in there?" Frank asked.

"A lot of junk a little too good to throw out," Jake answered. "Might as well let it burn."

"It's pretty far from the store," Frank said. "But you don't want the fire to spread."

"It sounded to me as if it started with an explosion. What do you suppose caused it?" Joe asked.

Jake shrugged and said, "I don't know. There might have been a couple of old five-gallon jerricans in there. You heat one of those up, and if there's a little gasoline left in it, the vapor can turn it into a bomb."

"So you think the fire came first, then the explosion?" Frank pursued.

"How do I know? I wasn't here. I was at that

meeting, same as everybody else," Jake said, sounding irritated. He took a couple of steps sideways and turned half away from the Hardys.

Joe looked over at Frank and rolled his eyes. After the fire was out, Joe and Frank went back to their cabin to talk over their investigation.

"The explosion has to be part of the pattern," Joe insisted. "And if it is, it means that the motive isn't to keep David from doing well in the race, the way we thought. It's to intimidate people who are against the ThemeLife project."

"Jake isn't against the project," Frank pointed out. "And it was his shed that blew up."

Joe thought for a few moments, then said, "What if the arsonist is out to make everybody realize how shaky their way of life is without something like the theme park? Then it wouldn't matter whether the target is someone like Peter, who's been speaking out against the project, or someone like Jake, who says he's neutral."

"That's a really nifty theory, Joe," Frank said. "And if the explosion *is* part of the pattern, we can narrow down our list of suspects . . . a little too much. Just about everybody in town was in the hall when the shed blew up."

"I didn't see Gregg there," Joe said.

"Or David," Frank added.

"Get real, Frank! You can't tell me you suspect David!"

"Of course not," Frank replied. "All I meant is, whether somebody was at the meeting doesn't tell us much. Jake might be right, that the explosion happened *after* the fire started. Or, if it was a bomb, it could have been set off by a timer. If that's so, then anyone could have been responsible, whether he was at the meeting or not."

Joe felt his spirits start to droop. For a moment he had been sure that they were near a solution, but now the answer to the mystery seemed as far away as ever.

He heard a knock on the door and opened it. David was standing there.

"I wanted to tell you," David said, after coming in and taking off his parka, "I got Big Foot back, unhurt."

"That's great!" Joe exclaimed.

"Yes, it is," David replied. "But I'm really upset. When I took Big Foot back to the kennel, I found out somebody had cut his tether rope."

Frank nodded. "We noticed that," he said. "I didn't have a chance to tell you."

"I can't believe Gregg would go that far," David continued, pacing up and down in the little cabin. "What does he want, to start a feud? He knows I could hurt his dogs as easily as he can hurt mine, and then we'd both be out of the running."

"Have you seen Gregg lately?" asked Joe. "We'd like to ask him some questions."

David shook his head. "He must be out training every minute he can. I'd do the same, but I've been distracted by the fire and everything else that's been happening. I'm nervous that my team is starting to lose its edge."

Early the next morning Frank and Joe went to look over the burnt-out ruin of Jake's storage shed. The charred timbers of the shack smelled sooty and acrid. Large cans were blackened and deformed by the heat. A metal bed frame sagged in the middle where the heat had softened the steel.

"What are we looking for?" Joe asked as he and Frank shifted a fallen roofbeam out of the way.

"Anything that looks out of place," Frank replied.

Joe chuckled. Pointing to the wreckage of an ancient snowmobile, he said, "With all this junk *nothing's* going to look out of place."

After twenty minutes of rummaging, Frank gave a triumphant shout. "Joe, look at this!"

Frank was holding the remains of an old-fashioned windup alarm clock.

"More junk," Joe said.

"Maybe," Frank said. "But look—there's a metal pin sticking through the face at twelve o'clock, with the minute hand touching it."

"I get it!" Joe exclaimed. "You run one wire to the minute hand and another to the pin, hook it up to a battery, and you've got a timer for a bomb!"

"Looks that way," Frank replied. "And I think I saw clocks like this on Jake's shelves. I wonder if he remembers selling one recently."

Joe said, "Come on, let's ask him."

Jake was sweeping the floor when Frank and Joe went into the store.

"Find anything?" Jake asked. "I saw you looking through the mess. I'll have to clear it up come spring."

"We found this," Frank said. He held out the burned clock.

"Oh, that," Jake said. "What about it? I must have thrown that out ten years ago."

"Nobody bought one of these clocks from you recently?" Joe asked.

"I wish they had," Jake replied, pointing to a row of identical clocks on the shelf. "This isn't the big city, you know. People in Glitter don't have much use for alarm clocks."

As the Hardys left the store, Frank saw Curt up the road, heading out of town. The ThemeLife official gave a furtive glance over his shoulder, as if checking whether anyone was watching him.

"What's he up to?" Joe asked.

"Let's find out," Frank said.

They let Curt get a good lead on them, then followed him. Five minutes later Joe said, "We know this road. The only thing out this way is Lucky's placer mine."

"Why is he going there?" Frank asked. "He already knows Lucky is voting for ThemeLife. Why waste time trying to persuade somebody who's already persuaded?"

"Good point," Joe said.

At the cabin Lucky opened the door before Curt had a chance to knock.

"It looks as if he was expected," Joe whispered. "Let's see if we can get close enough to hear what they're saying."

The two brothers crept around to the side of the cabin and positioned themselves on either side of a window.

They were just in time to hear Curt say, "I don't want any more of these fires and bombings. You hear?"

"Why tell me?" Lucky demanded in an angry voice.

"You're giving the company a bad image, and I want it stopped," Curt said.

Lucky started yelling. "Who do you think you are, coming out here and telling me what to do? I'll do what I want to do. If it's bombing and fires, then it's bombing and fires. If you and your big-deal company don't like it, you can go jump in the Yukon!"

Frank looked over at Joe and raised his eyebrows. It sounded as if one of their prime suspects had just confessed.

"Where'd you get the idea that you're helping the situation?" Curt continued. "We've got too much at stake to put up with this. If it doesn't stop, right now, *I'll* stop it. You hear?"

"You don't come onto my property and order *me* around," Lucky shouted.

Curt retorted, "I'm not ordering you around. But if you think I'm going to let some crazy old coot of a prospector ruin a multimillion-dollar project, you're wrong—dead wrong. Anything that has to be done, *I'm* the one who'll do it."

Frank and Joe looked at each other again. *Another* prime suspect had just confessed!

Frank stiffened. Something was moving through the underbrush behind them—something big. He looked over his shoulder and a chill ran down his spine.

A brown bear was lumbering out of the bushes. It stopped when it saw the Hardys. Then it reared up on its hind legs, bared its enormous white teeth, and let out a growl that rattled the window of the cabin.

"Oh, no," Frank said. "What do we do now?"

12 Dynamite Dealings

Joe straightened up slowly, keeping his eyes on the bear. He heard Curt, inside the cabin, ask fearfully, "What's that noise?"

"Nothing but a nosy old bear," Lucky told him. "Don't worry, I'll settle his sauce!"

Frank caught Joe's attention and pointed to a boulder near the back of the cabin.

Joe nodded. A moment later he heard the door of the cabin slam open. When the bear turned its head toward the door, Joe and Frank dashed to the boulder, where they were hidden from both Lucky and the bear.

"You see this rifle in my hands?" Lucky

shouted at the bear. "Now get out of here or I'll blast you to kingdom come."

The bear growled but didn't move.

"Yeeeooo!" Lucky shouted, "Git! Get outta here, you big lumbering lunk, or you're on your way to bear heaven, you hear me? Git!"

Huddled out of sight, Joe heard the bear growl again. This time the sound was lower and not as threatening.

"Git, I tell you!" Lucky yelled. A shot rang out. Joe heard the crunch of running paws in the snow and the crackle of low branches breaking as the bear ran into the woods.

Joe let out his breath. He had been afraid the bear would come toward the boulder.

"Okay, city boy," Lucky called to Curt. "You can come outside now. He's gone."

"Why didn't you shoot it?" Curt demanded.

"Because I don't like bear meat," Lucky replied. "Besides, we've known each other a long time. I'd get lonely out here without that stupid bear."

"I'm going to leave now. But remember what I said," Curt warned.

"You'd better remember what *I* said," Lucky replied.

Joe and Frank looked at each other as Curt's footsteps faded down the trail. After a long moment they heard Lucky's cabin door slam shut.

"Let's go," Joe whispered.

On the way back to town Joe said, "Well, Lucky isn't working for Curt. But he could still be the one doing all the sabotage on his own. Curt seems to think he is."

"But if Curt's the one," Frank replied, "he might accuse Lucky as a smoke screen."

"Why do that, unless there were other people to hear?" Joe objected. "Unless . . . Frank, do you think Curt knew we were following him? Maybe he and Lucky staged the whole thing for us."

Frank grinned. "Including the bear? I doubt it. Anyway, we still don't know for sure that all these incidents are linked to the ThemeLife plan. How is cutting Big Foot's tether going to get anybody to vote for the plan?"

Joe fell silent. He had to admit that Frank's question stumped him . . . for now, at least.

As the Hardys entered the town, they saw Justine coming up the hill. She had a bag of flour slung over one shoulder. She recognized them and waved, then put the bag on the ground and waited for them.

"Hi," she said, when they came up to her. "Listen, I just saw something. I don't know if it's important, but I thought I'd better tell you."

114

"What is it, Justine?" Frank asked.

Justine hesitated, then said, "I went by the post office to see if the mail plane had brought anything for us yesterday. Curt Stone was there, picking up his mail, too."

"When was this?" Joe asked. "We saw him a little while ago."

"It was just a few minutes ago," Justine said. "Anyway, he got a big stack of letters and started going through them. Then some other people came in, and he put down his letters to talk to them. That's when I saw it."

Frank asked, "Saw what, Justine? Something about one of the letters?"

She nodded. "I know I shouldn't have peeked," she said, turning pink. "It's just that this one word in the return address caught my eye."

Joe took a deep breath and asked, "What word, Justine?"

She looked at him from under her lashes and said, "Dynamite. The return address was the Northfield Dynamite Company, in Fairbanks. I noticed it because I couldn't think what Curt Stone would be doing getting a letter from a dynamite company. Is it important?"

Frank nodded. "It could be *very* important, Justine. Thanks for telling us."

"Oh, you're welcome," she said. "I'd better

go. This is Mom's baking day, and David's mother was out of flour." She picked up the bag, put it on her shoulder, and walked up the path.

Joe turned to Frank. "Why would Curt have any dealings with a dynamite company?" he asked.

"To blow things up?" Frank suggested. "If he's got a better reason, maybe we ought to find it out."

The Hardys walked through the town. Curt had to be around somewhere, and Glitter was too small for someone to stay out of sight for long.

They found Curt on the far side of town, coming out of a cabin.

"Hi, boys," he said when he saw them. "How're you liking Glitter? Are you starting to yearn for the bright lights?"

"It's pretty exciting around here," Frank said dryly. "Fires, explosions . . . That reminds me— have you ever heard of the Northfield Dynamite Company?"

Curt's face colored angrily, but he managed a smile. "Just as I said, news travels fast around here," he said. "Well, my snoopy friends, I never heard of the company before today. But today I heard *from* the company. Somebody in the post office noticed the envelope, I guess."

"They just wrote you out of the blue?" Joe asked.

"Right," Curt replied. "They sent me a price list."

"That's quite a coincidence, coming the day after Jake's shack blew up," Frank said.

"It's no coincidence at all. It's obviously part of a plot to discredit me and the ThemeLife Company. I never asked for that price list. I have no use for dynamite. If I did, I'd buy it from Jake."

Joe frowned. "Jake sells dynamite?"

"Jake sells everything from antiques to zebra-striped vests," Curt retorted. "Get it? A to Z? People around here need dynamite, for mining or blowing up stumps or settling arguments with their neighbors. So Jake sells it. Simple. See you later. Don't forget what too much curiosity did to the cat."

After Curt walked away, Joe asked, "Do you believe that story?"

"He makes it hard to believe him," Frank said. "But why would he admit getting that price list if it incriminates him? Everybody here has a wood stove. Open the fire door, toss the paper in, and there goes the evidence, up in smoke."

"So Jake sells dynamite," Joe said slowly. "I wonder whom he's sold it to lately."

"Let's go ask him," Frank suggested.

They were nearly to the store when Joe spotted

Jake down by the river, standing next to a weird, rickety-looking machine. "There he is," he said.

He and Frank walked down the path to the riverbank. When they were a few yards away, Joe called out, "Hi, Jake."

The storekeeper jumped, then turned to face them. "Hello," he said. "You startled me. I didn't hear you coming."

Frank nodded toward the machine. "What on earth is that thing?" he asked.

Jake glanced over his shoulder. "That's a fishwheel," he said. "Come summer, the river current turns the paddlewheel, and those chicken-wire baskets dip down, scoop salmon out of the river, and drop them into a slatted box. Whole thing works automatically."

"That's pretty clever," Joe said. "Is it yours?"

"No, no," Jake said. "It belongs to Ralph Hunter. I came down here because I thought I saw somebody lurking around it. After what happened to Ralph's boat the other day, I wasn't going to take any chances."

"Did you see who it was?" Joe asked.

Jake hesitated, then said, "I didn't get a good look, but I had a feeling it was Lucky Moeller."

Joe and Frank spent a few moments studying the fishwheel, then walked back to the store with Jake and asked him about dynamite.

"I haven't sold any since fall," he said, giving

them a shrewd glance. "You boys are thinking about that shed of mine, aren't you? I doubt it was dynamited. You wouldn't have seen anything left big enough to make toothpicks. No, I'd say it caught fire somehow, and one of those jerricans I was storing blew up." He went up onto the porch, then turned and said, "Still, it *could* have been dynamite."

As the Hardys walked up the hill toward their cabin, Joe said, "I don't see how Lucky could have gotten from his mine to that fishwheel in time. He would have had to pass us on the trail. Maybe we haven't solved this case yet, but we're not dumb enough to miss someone running past us on a deserted road!"

"Jake must have been mistaken," Frank replied. "Unless . . . it's no secret that he and Lucky dislike each other. Maybe Jake made it up, to get Lucky in trouble."

"But he *was* down at the fishwheel," Joe objected. "Why would he leave his store and traipse down there if he didn't see someone acting suspiciously?"

"*Someone*," Frank said emphatically. "There's no proof it was Lucky. And we know one thing— it wasn't Curt. We were talking to him at the time Jake must have spotted the intruder."

From around a bend in the trail, Joe heard frantic barking and "Hike, hike!" Seconds later

Gregg's dogteam came racing around the curve. Joe and Frank stepped to the side, just off the packed-down part of the trail. Frank raised his hand, signaling Gregg to stop before he reached them.

Gregg called out again, "Hike, hike!" The powerful dogs increased their speed and kept running straight down the trail toward Joe and Frank.

The lead dog, teeth bared in threat, was only yards away when Joe realized the trail was too narrow.

The sled was going to crash into them.

13 The Process of Elimination

Frank swept out his left arm and pushed Joe off the trail, then jumped back himself. Joe tripped on a chunk of ice and tumbled into the snow, but Frank stayed on his feet.

"Gregg!" he shouted. "We need—"

Gregg's answer was to aim his gloved fist at Frank's face as he went by.

Frank snapped. Gritting his teeth, he grabbed Gregg's wrist with both hands and twisted. Taken by surprise, Gregg flew off the back of the dogsled and landed hard in the middle of the trail. His team, alerted by the sudden change in their payload, slowed down and came to a stop a few yards down the trail.

Gregg was stunned by his fall. He sat up slowly, rubbing the back of his head, and looked defiantly from Frank to Joe.

Frank was still mad. "Listen, turkey," he said. "Just what is your problem? That's the second time you've tried to run us down. And whenever something bad's happened in Glitter, you've been somewhere in the picture. Right after the Windman cabin caught fire, you went sledding off into the sunset. You brought Peter and Mona that basket of poisoned fruit. You were practically the only person in the town who wasn't at the meeting yesterday when somebody bombed Jake's shed. And I would personally like to know where you were when some lowlife cut the tether on one of David's team and let Big Foot run away."

"You talk!" Gregg said scornfully. "Who threw drugged meat in my kennel? Who cut my harness half through? Who put sand in my runner wax?"

Joe replied, "I give up. Who?"

Gregg struggled to his feet. "You did! David's gangster friends from New York! He brought you here to help him beat me in the Iditarod, didn't he? And you'll do anything to make it happen. But I won't let you ruin my dream! Never!"

Taken aback, Frank looked over at Joe, who was just as surprised by this turn of events. Were Gregg's accusations some kind of bluff? Or was

Gregg, too, a target of sabotage? And if so, who was responsible and why was the person doing it?

"Are you saying that all these things happened to you in the past couple of days, since we came to Glitter?" Frank demanded.

Gregg hesitated. "There were accidents before," he said slowly, "but those were David's fault."

Joe asked, "How do you know?"

"Who else?" Gregg retorted. "We used to be friends once, but how can I stay friends with someone who tries to harm my dogs and wreck my life?"

Frank put every ounce of sincerity he could into his voice as he said, "Gregg, someone's been trying to hurt David, too. Someone's trying to destroy your whole town. David and Peter and Mona asked us to find out who it is."

"We're not gangsters," Joe added. "We're detectives."

Hope and disbelief struggled on Gregg's face. Disbelief won. "Now you're trying to confuse me," he said. "Where is your proof?"

"We don't have any yet," Frank admitted. "But when we do, you'll see that we're telling you the truth. David isn't your enemy."

Gregg gave Frank a searching look. Then, without a word, he turned and walked down the path to where his dog team waited patiently.

"He didn't believe us," Joe said. "But he wanted to."

Frank nodded. "I know. The question is, do we believe him? If the answer's yes, then we just lost one of our main suspects."

"I think I do," Joe said slowly. "Unless he's an awfully good actor . . ."

Still discussing Gregg, the Hardys continued up the track and decided to drop in on the Windmans. They knocked on the door, and Mona opened it.

"Oh," she said, holding up a length of striped wool. "I thought you were Lucky. He forgot his scarf. Come on in."

"Lucky was here?" Joe asked, after he and Frank took off their parkas. "When?"

"Why, just now," Mona replied. "Why?"

"Was he here long?" Frank asked.

From his seat near the stove Peter said, "About fifteen minutes. He was trying to talk me into supporting the ThemeLife project. He even offered me a job as a tour guide at his mine," he added with a chuckle.

The door flew open. Lucky came in so fast he seemed to bring the wind with him. Snow fell off his boots and made puddles on the floor. "My scarf," he said. "I nigh froze my neck without it."

124

Laughing, Mona handed it to him. He wrapped it around twice and turned to leave.

"Lucky?" Frank said quickly. "Were you down by Ralph Hunter's fishwheel? Jake said he saw you there."

"What? When?" Lucky demanded.

"Less than half an hour ago," Joe told him.

Lucky's face turned red. "He's lying through his teeth!" he shouted. "I haven't been down that way all day."

Peter looked puzzled. "How could Jake have seen Lucky down there?" he asked. "He was here with us. Jake must have made a mistake."

"It's easy to get people confused in winter," Mona added. "Everybody's so bundled up."

"That must be it," Frank said.

"Anything wrong with Ralph's fishwheel?" Lucky asked suspiciously.

"Not that we know of," Joe replied.

"Because if something *does* go wrong with it," Lucky continued, "you won't have to look far to know who to blame. That lying, gouging, money-grubber Jake Ferguson, that's who!"

He stomped out, slamming the cabin door behind him.

Peter looked over at Frank and Joe and said, "Would you believe that, under that gruff exterior, Lucky is a kind, considerate friend? No? I didn't think so. Half the time I don't believe it myself. But it's true, just the same."

The door opened, and Justine came in with an armload of firewood. When she saw Frank and Joe, she said, "Hi. Did you find out about the dynamite?"

Peter and Mona looked surprised. Frank told them about the envelope Justine had seen, then gave them Curt's explanation. "He could have been lying," Frank concluded. "But I can't figure out why he'd risk getting mail from a dynamite company if he's mixed up in criminal activity."

"Everything that's happened is so confusing," Peter said, rubbing his forehead. "I hope you can straighten it out before it wrecks our community."

"Speaking of the community," Mona said, "tomorrow is a big day here, and we want you to be part of it."

"What's happening?" Joe asked.

"It's a ceremony we have every year," she explained. "A potlatch, with singing and dancing and a big feast to celebrate the return of spring."

The next morning Joe and Frank were out for a walk when they spotted Peter and David at the foot of a hill on the outskirts of town. Peter waved for the Hardys to join them. They all hiked up the hill to a clearing surrounded by a rail fence.

Joe spotted a headstone just inside the gate, poking through the snow, and realized this was the town cemetery.

Willy Ekus was there, staring at a headstone. When he saw Peter, he turned and left the cemetery, keeping a careful distance from them. That reminded Joe that he and Frank had suspected Willy of setting Peter's cabin on fire. Yet afterward Willy had dropped out of sight and out of their thoughts. Had he been lurking about the past two days, carrying on a campaign of sabotage?

When he got a chance, Joe took David aside and asked him about Willy.

"He's been away," David replied. "He has a valuable trapline up on the Mink River—*not* the one he and Uncle Peter keep arguing over. Every week he takes his team up there and spends a couple of days checking and resetting his traps."

Joe relayed this information to Frank later. "So, if it checks out," he concluded, "we'll have to cross Willy off our list, too. That list is getting awfully short."

"That's called the process of elimination," Frank pointed out. "It means we're getting somewhere."

"Unless we run out of suspects," Joe retorted. "Then it's called getting nowhere!"

* * *

That afternoon Frank and Joe joined the townspeople at the potlatch in the assembly room. A group of Athabascans stood up to sing in their native language, moving their bent hands and forearms up and down in front of them in time to the hypnotic chanting. Others shuffled their feet in a dance, turning slowly to the steady rhythms.

When the dance was over, the oldest member of the group spoke about the meaning of the day. When he was finished, two Athabascan women in traditional dress came forward. One was carrying a caldron, and the other carried a stack of bowls and a ladle. They went up to each person in turn and handed him or her a bowl of steaming broth.

"What's that?" Joe asked David in an undertone.

David grinned. "A ceremonial soup," he said. "Everybody must taste it. It's the custom."

Joe glanced at Frank, then asked, "What's in it?"

David's grin widened. "Moose head," he replied. "It's really good."

"It's made with a real moose head?" Frank asked.

David nodded, then said, "Don't worry, it's just for flavor. You'll like it."

The two women reached Joe and handed him a bowl. He gulped, then raised it and took a sip.

He wouldn't say he liked it, but it wasn't nearly as bad as he had expected. He tasted salt more than anything else.

He looked around the room. Everyone else seemed to be polishing off the soup and wanting more. Then something caught his eye.

"Frank?" he whispered. "I just saw Jake going out the door with a sneaky look on his face. I think we should see what he's up to."

"Right," Frank replied. "David, we've got something we have to do. We'll be right back."

"Was the soup that bad?" David asked, smiling.

"We'll explain later," Joe said, dragging Frank toward the door.

The Hardys followed Jake toward the west end of town and saw him vanish behind one of the cabins.

"Let's get up on that rise behind the cabin," Joe suggested. "We'll be able to see him from there."

They ran up through a band of trees, then crawled to the edge of a low cliff and looked over. The roof and rear wall of the cabin looked almost close enough to touch.

"What's he doing?" Frank whispered.

Joe narrowed his eyes. Jake was standing at the back of the cabin, near the door, glancing around suspiciously. He reached up and snatched two pairs of snowshoes hanging from a peg. He tucked them under his left arm, then reached inside his parka and tossed something down on the ground.

"He's stealing those snowshoes!" Frank declared. "What a slimeball!"

"What did he drop?" Joe asked. "We're too far up. I can't see." He moved forward to get a better look. But his hands slipped on the ice at the edge of the drop. He slid forward, over the cliff.

14 Setting the Trap

Frank heard Joe cry out. He turned his head just in time to see Joe slide past him on the steep, ice-coated slope. With lightning-fast reflexes, Frank darted out his right hand and grabbed Joe's left ankle as he went over the cliff. He felt the force of Joe's weight start to pull him toward the edge. Frantically he dug the toes of his boots into the snow but failed to get a grip. He felt himself sliding forward.

Just as it looked as if he and Joe were both going to plummet to the rocks thirty feet below, Frank managed to hook his left foot around the trunk of a small cedar. The tree bent with the strain, but the roots held.

"Hang on, Joe," Frank called. "I'll pull you back up."

"Hurry! I think I'm going to pass out."

Frank managed to clamp his left hand on Joe's ankle, taking some of the strain off his right arm. Contracting his abdominal muscles, he inched backward, towing Joe after him. Joe managed to get his other foot up, and Frank grabbed his right ankle and pulled Joe half onto the cliff. Joe clawed the ice with his hands, elbows, and knees, holding on to his precarious purchase on life.

Finally Frank was able to kneel, and with one last tug he pulled Joe all the way up over the edge. The two brothers sprawled, arms outstretched and chests heaving, and tried to catch their breaths.

"Whew. Thanks, bro," Joe said. "I thought I was going to skydive without a parachute."

"You know Dad would have a fit if you tried something that dumb," Frank said. He clapped Joe on the shoulder.

"Jake dropped something," Joe said, "just before I went over the edge."

"I know. I couldn't see what it was. Do you feel okay?"

Joe stood up. "Let's go see."

They made their way carefully down the slope. When they reached the back of the cabin,

Frank bent down and picked up a hammer. "Look," he said. "It's got *LM* scratched into the wood of the handle."

Joe peered at the tool and said, *"LM*—Lucky Moeller."

"Jake stole the snowshoes and planted the hammer here so Lucky would get the blame," Frank said.

"I bet this cabin belongs to someone who's spoken out against the ThemeLife project, too."

"That's the pattern," Frank agreed. "Are you thinking what I'm thinking?"

"You mean, that Jake's the bad guy we're after?" Joe replied. "It sure looks that way. And I'll tell you something else. I bet we came along yesterday just in time to save Ralph's fishwheel from being vandalized the same way his boat was."

"You're probably right," Frank said. "The problem is, we don't have a bit of evidence against him. We saw him take those snowshoes, but that's it. It's not enough."

"Do you have a plan?" Joe asked.

Frank stroked his chin. "Not quite . . . but I'm starting to get a glimmer of one."

The Hardys walked back to the assembly hall. The potlatch was breaking up.

"Follow my lead," Frank muttered to Joe.

133

The two brothers walked up to Curt. "Can we talk to you privately?" Frank asked him in a low voice.

Curt gave them a measuring look, then nodded. "I'll meet you at my cabin in ten minutes," he said.

At Curt's cabin Frank started the discussion by saying, "You know, a lot of people are blaming you and your company for the disasters the people of Glitter have been having recently."

"That's completely unfair," Curt said. "My company and I have nothing to do with them, nothing at all."

"ThemeLife has a fine reputation," Frank said. "And my brother and I believe you're innocent. We can give you a way of proving it—help us trap the real culprit."

"But you're just kids," Curt said. "How—"

"We may be young, but Joe and I have solved quite a few cases. Our father is well known in the investigative field. You can ask David Natik about us—he's seen my family at work before, and he's asked us to help him."

"David's a good man," Curt said, "from a good family—even if they do oppose the ThemeLife plan. I want this business cleared up. It's only right, and besides, my job's on the line."

Frank gave Joe a significant glance. They knew that if Curt had objected to helping trap the bad guy, it might have meant Curt had hired Jake to do his dirty work. His willingness to help them made that less likely.

"Great!" Joe said. "Let's go get him."

Curt stared at him. "You know who it is?"

Joe nodded. "Jake Ferguson," he said.

"That—" Curt exclaimed. "So he's the one! Well, I can't say I'm surprised. Do you know that Jake's been cornering the market in traditional crafts around here? He gives easy credit to people, then when they're up to their ears in debt, he takes the beaded mukluks and other Athabascan relics they've inherited to clear the slate. He's got stuff socked away that any museum would pay a fortune to have."

"So that's why he's doing everything he can to get the town to vote yes," Joe said. "If Glitter becomes a theme park, he'll make a bundle showing his collection and selling reproductions to tourists. The craftspeople who owe him money will have to make the copies for pennies. What a racket!"

"Listen, Curt," Frank said. "Here's what we'd like you to do. Write a note to Jake on your letterhead. Tell him you appreciate his activities on behalf of your company and you'd like to talk about closer cooperation. Set up a meeting."

Curt pursed his lips and shook his head. "If anyone found out about it, I'd be in real trouble.

135

My note would be proof that I support his criminal activities. No way, boys. Sorry."

"The note won't say anything about sabotage," Joe pointed out. "'Activities' could just mean telling people the plan's a good thing for the town."

"You won't be incriminating yourself at all," Frank added as persuasively as he could. "Jake will understand what the note means."

"It's a big risk," Curt said.

"We're going to catch Jake, sooner or later," Frank said. "What if he decides to throw all the blame on you and ThemeLife? Everybody will believe him. This way you'll have proof you're not part of his plot."

Curt frowned and said, "I see your point, Frank. I can't say I like it, but I'll go along with you."

He took out a sheet of ThemeLife letterhead and started writing. "When and where?" he asked.

Frank looked around. Curt's cabin was as small as the one he and Joe were sharing. Curt had set up the living area as an office. He also had a sleeping alcove and a tiny kitchen in the corner. The windows were small and double paned against the cold. He doubted he and Joe could hear a conversation if they stood outside.

He glanced up and saw a loft over the kitchen

and sleeping alcove. "Is there any room up there?" he asked Curt, and pointed to the loft.

"I guess so," Curt replied. "I've never looked. I'm just renting this place month to month. If ThemeLife goes through and I'm assigned to run it, I'll probably build my own cabin."

Frank and Joe climbed the narrow ladder to the loft. Behind a stack of old cartons and casks was an empty space about four feet by six. It was hidden from anyone standing below.

"Perfect," Frank called to Curt. "Write down that you'll meet him here in an hour and a half. That'll give us time to make our preparations."

A little over an hour later Joe studied the intent faces around him in the loft. He and Frank had talked Peter, David, and Gregg into joining them as witnesses. David and Gregg were still awkward with each other, but Joe could tell they were both glad to have found out their suspicions weren't true. They wanted to be friends again, and Joe had a hunch they'd succeed.

Curt was downstairs. Joe heard him cough and rustle some papers. Unless Jake insisted on whispering, those in the loft would hear every word clearly.

If Jake showed up. . . .

The group sat down on the floor to wait. Frank looked at his watch, then met Joe's eyes. Would

Curt's note be enough bait to pull the wily storekeeper in? That phrase about closer cooperation—would Jake read that to mean a payoff, as they'd intended him to? Frank had hoped Curt would have said he wanted to reimburse Jake for his efforts. But Frank understood why Curt had refused to take the risk. What if his note ended up being read in court?

The minutes dragged on. What if Jake had been keeping an eye on Curt's cabin and had seen them all arrive? He'd know then that Curt's letter was intended to draw him into a trap. And even if he hadn't seen them, he was sure to be suspicious of Curt's summons. Peter had insisted on sweeping away their footprints in the snow, but had he done a thorough enough job?

To distract himself, Joe tried reciting in his mind "The Shooting of Dan McGrew" by Robert W. Service, the Canadian poet who wrote about the north country. How did it begin? Something about a cold winter evening? He jumped when Gregg, who was seated next to him, touched him on the shoulder and put his fingers to his lips. Joe realized he'd been reciting aloud. What if Jake had come in and heard him?

Not that it looked as if there was much chance of that. Where was Jake anyway? Joe was beginning to think he wouldn't show up. Then he heard a knock on the door. His companions stilled their movements and waited.

Joe heard Curt's footsteps as he crossed the room. The cabin door creaked open.

"Hi, Jake," Curt said. "Glad you could come. What's the rifle for—going hunting?"

Joe glanced at the others. Their grave faces showed they understood Jake was armed.

"I don't believe in taking chances, that's all," Jake said.

Curt said, "Good. Neither do I. I'm not taking any chances that my company's plan might be turned down because of a few agitators. And I think we can work together. Let's sit down and talk about it."

Frank took out a microcassette recorder, ready to tape what Curt and Jake said. He pressed the Record button. The noise the machine made was faint, but Jake heard the click.

"Hey, what was that?" he asked, and scraped back his chair.

Then Joe heard the *snick* of a rifle's being cocked.

15 Hometown Champions

Frank froze. If Jake came up to the loft, he'd see them. Their plan would be ruined, and they'd be face-to-face with an angry and desperate man who had a rifle. Rather than run that risk, Frank decided he'd attack Jake the instant he started up the ladder. With surprise as his ally, he was sure he could overpower Jake.

"What are you doing?" he heard Curt ask. "Will you put that thing down? And put the safety back on. Guns make me nervous."

"I heard something," Jake said. "It came from up there."

"Mice," Curt said. "This cabin's full of them. I'm half tempted to take something off the rent

140

because of it. Now, can we get down to business?"

Frank heard Jake uncock the rifle, then a chair scraped on the floor. He must have gone back to his seat. Frank took a deep breath and let it out. The recorder was still on, the tape turning silently. Frank placed the recorder on the floor and hoped the tape wouldn't run out too soon.

"What kind of business did you have in mind?" Jake asked cautiously. "Your note was kind of vague."

"Let's not beat around the bush," Curt replied. "I figured out what you've been up to. I wouldn't have thought of it myself, but I can tell it's persuading people to vote my way, so I'm all for it."

"Uh-huh," Jake said. "Glad to hear it. So?"

"So, I want you to know that ThemeLife is ready to pay your expenses and a sizable bonus for keeping up the pressure on the people who are trying to get in the way of progress."

"A sizable bonus," Jake said in a thoughtful tone. "When?"

"Right after the voters of Glitter approve the ThemeLife proposal," Curt told him. "Your expense money you can get as we go along. What do you say?"

"It's a deal," Jake said.

Frank caught Joe's eye and grinned. The fish

had just snapped at the bait. Now all Curt had to do was set the hook and reel him in.

Curt's tone changed. "I wonder . . ." he said. "I'm not a hundred percent sure you're the man I want."

Jake's voice rose. "What do you mean, not the man you want!"

"I'm just wondering, that's all," Curt said. "Are you really the one who did all those things?"

"Of course I am!" Jake said. "Who else?"

Curt sounded skeptical. "Why would you blow up your own building?"

Jake laughed. "Because nobody would think I would blow up my own building, that's why. They'd think someone else was doing all this stuff. It put me in the clear. Besides, that old shack was about to fall down anyway."

"And Peter Windman's cabin?" Curt continued.

In the loft Peter stirred. His face was taut, and his fists were clenched. Frank shot him a quick warning glance, and he settled back.

"Easy as pie," Jake boasted. "I just dropped a Mason jar of gasoline through the back window, near the stove, and threw in a match.

"Then, after they settled in at the Natik place," he added, "I flung a log through the window, just to keep them on edge. That Peter's been talking to too many people, working them up against the plan."

"So you broke into his cache and stole his meat supply, too?" Curt asked.

"Say, you've really been keeping track, haven't you?" Jake said. "Sure, that was me. And I wrecked Ralph Hunter's longboat, too. I just waited till nobody was around, then went to work with a hammer and big spike. *Whack! Whack! Whack!* Didn't take me long at all."

Curt said, "One thing I don't understand is why you went after Gregg's dog team. His dad hasn't said anything against ThemeLife."

Jake laughed, a low sound that gave Frank shivers. "That was really a smart touch," he said. "See, I'm planning to get at Peter through his nephew, David. I already started, by letting one of David's best dogs loose. But then it came to me. If I pull a few tricks on Gregg, too, everybody will think that the two kids are feuding with each other. They'll never suspect me."

This was too much for Gregg. He jumped to his feet and ran down the ladder. "You skunk!" he shouted. "You tried to poison my dogs! I'll kill you for that!"

Frank stood up and looked over the barricade of cartons. Jake had grabbed his rifle and was aiming it at Gregg.

"Hold it right there, or I'll put daylight

through you," Jake told Gregg. His voice was trembling. He looked over at Curt and added, "And you—you set a trap for me. I'll settle with you, see if I don't!"

Curt's face turned pale. "You can't get away now," he said. He backed away from Jake.

"Why not?" Jake asked. The rifle barrel moved in a little circle, covering Curt as well as Gregg. "All I've got to do is shoot both of you and make it look like you shot each other. Everyone'll think that Gregg figured out you'd messed with his dog team and came after you."

Frank's eyes widened. Jake thought that Curt and Gregg were the only other people in the cabin! Frank made an urgent gesture to Joe, David, and Peter to keep absolutely still.

"Now, let's see," Jake said. He sounded as if he was starting to enjoy himself. "Which of you should I plug first? Curt, I think, for trying to double-cross me."

He raised the rifle and aimed it Curt. Frank took a deep breath and launched himself from the edge of the loft. At that same moment Joe gave the sharp, high-pitched shout of a martial arts expert.

Startled and distracted, Jake swung the rifle around. But before he could bring it to bear, Frank cannoned into him and knocked him to the floor.

There was a deafening noise right next to Frank's ear. Though partly stunned, he got to his knees, grabbed Jake by the front of his shirt, and gave him a solid right to the jaw. Jake's eyes rolled upward, and he slumped back to the floor.

Frank stumbled to his feet, picked up Jake's rifle, and looked around. "Anybody hurt?" he called.

Peter, David, and Joe rushed down the ladder. "No, we're fine," Joe said. "The bullet hit the ceiling."

"And you all heard what Jake said, right?" Frank asked.

Peter came over and stared down at the groggy Jake. "We sure did," he said. "And we're ready to repeat it in court, too."

"You hear that, Jake?" Joe said. He waved the recorder. "Your goose is cooked."

David laughed and said, "You're in the Alaskan bush now, Joe. Up here we say, Your *moose* is cooked!"

The next morning a plane from the Alaska state police flew up from Fairbanks and landed on the river. Two troopers handcuffed Jake, took statements from all the witnesses, and pocketed Frank's tape.

"Congratulations," one of the troopers said to Frank and Joe before taking Jake off to jail. "That was good, solid detective work. I wouldn't be surprised if our commander will want to send you a testimonial letter."

Later that day Curt called a meeting of the townspeople in the assembly room. "I've learned a lot in the last few months," he told them. "I've seen the pride you have in your way of life. I still believe that my company's plan will help preserve that way of life, not destroy it, but I respect those of you who disagree."

He paused and looked over to where Peter, Mona, Justine, and David were sitting. "I'd also like to announce that I spoke to the home office of ThemeLife this morning. Even though we had no responsibility for the damage, the company is going to rebuild the Windmans' cabin and replace Ralph Hunter's boat."

Everyone clapped and cheered. When the applause died down, Curt added, with a twinkle in his eye, "I've also asked the grocer in Fairbanks to send up his biggest basket of fresh fruit for the town. And I will personally test each piece of fruit myself!"

As everybody laughed, Peter jumped to his feet and said, "Thanks, Curt. I've been giving a great deal of thought to the ThemeLife plan. I've never been against you, and I appreciate what you did to smoke out Jake. I'm beginning to think you and the town can work together to bring

146

modern amenities to Glitter without destroying our way of life."

A murmur rippled through the crowd. Peter held up his hand. "We've got a lot to discuss, and I'm not saying for sure I'll vote for ThemeLife until we find out more."

"I'm glad to hear it," Curt said. "Let's talk later."

"That'll be fine," Peter said. "But for now, I think the whole town ought to give a vote of thanks to Frank and Joe Hardy, whose wonderful detective work saved our town from Jake. His greed would have destroyed us. We must never allow ourselves to be greedy."

The townspeople cheered, although a few shook their heads in disbelief at Peter's change of heart.

Frank felt his cheeks get warm as all at once the townspeople surged to their feet, applauding him and his brother. He knew these people would make it.

On Friday morning Frank and Joe helped David move his team, sled, and supplies out onto the river next to the landing strip. Gregg and his team were already there.

Justine was petting Gregg's lead dog, which bared its teeth at Ironheart as soon as he saw him. Justine pulled back, but Ironheart gave a loud

147

sniff and ignored his rival. David laughed and reached down to ruffle his fur.

Joe glanced over his shoulder. It looked as if the entire population of Glitter was coming onto the ice to join them. What had someone said? It was ten feet thick? Was that thick enough? No one else seemed concerned.

"Uh, David?" he said. "That's an awfully big crowd."

"Don't worry Joe, the ice can hold it."

"I didn't mean that," Joe said. "I was just wondering whether the plane would have enough room for everybody."

"Don't sweat it, Joe," David said. "Uncle Peter called Flip yesterday to let him know there'd be two dog teams and a lot of passengers flying out today. They're sending two big planes. Besides, most of these people are here to see us off. They're not coming with us."

"Hey, David," Gregg called. "I want to wish you luck in the Iditarod," he said.

"Thanks, Gregg. The same to you. We've got to make Glitter proud of us."

Joe heard the hum of an engine in the distance. He looked up and saw a dot in the sky. "There's the first plane," he said.

Peter and Mona joined the group.

"I know there's not much chance that either

148

you or I will come in first," David said. "It's the first time we're running the race, after all."

"But we'll give it our best shot." Gregg slapped David on the shoulder. "Won't we?"

"Sure, you will," said Curt, who arrived in time to hear Gregg and David. He turned to the crowd. "Hey, people, let's give three cheers for Gregg, David, and their two champion teams." The people clapped and shouted. Mona hugged David.

"And three more for Frank and Joe Hardy!" Justine called, and ran over and hugged each one in turn.

More clapping and shouting. After the noise died down, Joe raised his hands over his head and said, "Thanks, everybody. It's been great coming to Glitter and getting to know you. Frank and I are going to be at the Iditarod starting line in Anchorage, cheering on your hometown champions. We'll be thinking of all of you." He winked at Justine.

"And may the best dogs win!" Frank cried.

R·L·STINE'S
GHOSTS of FEAR STREET ®

1 HIDE AND SHRIEK   52941-2/$3.99

2 WHO'S BEEN SLEEPING IN MY GRAVE?
52942-0/$3.99

3 THE ATTACK OF THE AQUA APES
52943-9/$3.99

4 NIGHTMARE IN 3-D   52944-7/$3.99

5 STAY AWAY FROM THE TREEHOUSE
52945-5/$3.99

6 EYE OF THE FORTUNETELLER 52946-3/$3.99

7 FRIGHT KNIGHT   52947-1/$3.99

8 THE OOZE   52948-X/$3.99

9 REVENGE OF THE SHADOW PEOPLE
52949-8/$3.99

Available from Minstrel® Books
Published by Pocket Books

POCKET
BOOKS

Simon & Schuster Mail Order Dept. BWB
200 Old Tappan Rd., Old Tappan, N.J. 07675

Please send me the books I have checked above. I am enclosing $_____(please add $0.75 to cover the postage and handling for each order. Please add appropriate sales tax). Send check or money order--no cash or C.O.D.'s please. Allow up to six weeks for delivery. For purchase over $10.00 you may use VISA: card number, expiration date and customer signature must be included.

Name _____

Address _____

City _____ State/Zip _____

VISA Card # _____ Exp.Date _____

Signature _____

1146-07

NANCY DREW® MYSTERY STORIES By Carolyn Keene

A MINSTREL® BOOK

Published by Pocket Books

Simon & Schuster, Mail Order Dept. HB5, 200 Old Tappan Rd., Old Tappan, N.J. 07675
Please send me copies of the books checked. Please add appropriate local sales tax.
- [ ] Enclosed full amount per copy with this coupon (Send check or money order only)
- [ ] If order is $10.00 or more, you may charge to one of the following accounts: [ ] Mastercard [ ] Visa
Please be sure to include proper postage and handling: 0.95 for first copy; 0.50 for each additional copy ordered.
Name _____
Address _____
City _____ State/Zip _____
Credit Card # _____ Exp.Date _____
Signature _____
Books listed are also available at your bookstore. Prices are subject to change without notice.

760-20